I0563251

Fallen Hero

Firehouse Blues Series: Book 6

AE Moran

The Invisible Publishing Company

Firehouse Blues Series

Contents

Chapter 1: Sophie

I walk into a wall of noise in the Howe Firehouse training room.

Everyone stands up unlike every other staff training session I've been to. The crew's agitated voices send a wave of tension through the room.

I go over to a cluster of firefighters and paramedics standing on one side. I don't even get a chance to ask what's wrong.

"This better not be another shakedown," Billy Cates growls under his breath.

"Since when did John ever shake us down?" Caleb Watts asks. "We're here for training just like we always are."

"Then why are all the chairs lined up across the room?" Keith Brewer waves at the rows of chairs behind him. "This place is set up for a staff meeting, but we just had one last week. We aren't scheduled for another one for at least a week. I agree with Billy. Something fishy is going on."

"Maybe John is getting ready to hand out the latest round of awards and decorations,' Ellis Barrett suggests.

"Don't get all bright and cheery about that," Danny Brewer tells him. "No one is gonna pin any medals on you, munchkin."

"That's because you always take them for yourself," Ellis counters.

"If we aren't here for training and we aren't here for a staff meeting, why are we here?" Naomi McFee asks.

"It better not be a disciplinary hearing or anything like that," Billy growls again.

Chris Daniels turns to me. "You haven't heard anything about this, have you, Sophie? Do you know why we're here?"

"How could I know if you don't?" I ask. "I got the memo the same way all of you do. If Keith and Danny don't know, I don't see how any of us could know."

"That's the whole point, see?" Keith points out. "John must be keeping this a secret if he didn't even tell his own brothers. Something weird is going on."

"You said that before," Danny tells him.

Keith glares at him, but right then, Fire Chief John Brewer walks into the training room.

The noise level surges off the charts the minute he crosses the threshold.

Everyone steps forward and mobs him while they bombard him with a million questions. I can't hear a thing over all the noise.

He finally raises his hands and yells to make himself heard over all the other voices in the room. "Quiet down, all of you!"

The commotion dies down only slightly.

"Everyone take your seats so we can get started," he goes on.

"Get started on what?" Keith asks.

"When are you going to tell us what's going on?" Caleb asks. "Why are you being so secretive about this meeting?"

"It better not be something bad," Billy mutters.

"If we're here to receive decorations, just tell us now," Danny chimes in.

"All you care about is decorations," Chris teases.

Danny gives her a dirty look, but John interrupts. "If you all sit down like I told you to, I might be able to explain this......"

Another tide of questions launches at him from all over the room. I haven't seen the fire crew this worked up in a long, long time.

John tries to field a dozen questions and remarks at the same time, but he eventually loses patience again.

"Sit down and be quiet!" he bellows. "Anyone still standing in ten seconds is going to get written up in your files with a formal reprimand."

People finally start to drift away to their seats, but not without plenty of grumbling, mumbling, and more questions, threats, and dark glances cast over their shoulders in John's direction.

He sighs, passes his hand across his eyes, and continues to the front of the room like he originally planned to when he walked in here.

I take my seat near Naomi, Chris, and Brooke Elsworth.

The other firefighters keep muttering to themselves while John places a stack of file folders on the table at the front of the room.

I recognize these files. They're case files on incident reports and medical records. He usually keeps these in his office.

Now I know this isn't a normal staff meeting. He never brings files like that to staff meetings or training sessions. This must be serious.

He messes around with the overhead display equipment for a minute while he waits for all of us to settle down. He hooks up his laptop to the monitor and fiddles with it to turn it on.

Ellis cuts the tension by speaking up first. "What is this all about, man? Don't leave us in suspense. Is someone getting fired or something?"

John finally straightens up and faces us. "No one is getting fired and none of you is in trouble. I want to make that clear right from the start."

"Now I'm really worried," Caleb adds. "You know you're in trouble when the boss says none of you is in trouble."

That sets off another cascade of comments from the peanut gallery. John raises his hands again. "Will you all just shut up for a second?! Jesus, how many times do I have to say it?"

He gets a slight response, but the tension in the crowd doesn't fade at all.

He takes a deep breath. "The State Health and Safety Commission has been looking into all our recent injuries and deaths—among our crew and among our patients." He raises his hands again. "No one is saying any of that was your fault. The Commission just wants to make sure we have adequate health and safety procedures, protocols, and protections in place so you can all do your jobs without getting hurt."

"Working on the fire crew is dangerous. We all understand that," Josh Abbot points out. "We could get hurt even if we do have adequate health and safety procedures in place."

"And we're going out to deal with people who are already suffering from life-threatening injuries and illnesses," Naomi adds. "Some of them are going to die. There isn't a lot we can do about that."

"I'm not talking about that," John replies. "I'm talking about that car rolling on top of Ellen. I'm talking about Billy getting run over and little Georgie getting killed at the scene. I'm talking about Chris and Josh getting trapped in a burning building. I'm talking about that ceiling caving in on Keith and Leila." He raises his stack of files. "I have a laundry list of injuries that could have cost some of you your lives and, in some cases, actually did cost patients their lives. The State Commission is sending us a new Health and Safety officer who will audit....."

He doesn't get the rest of the words out before the whole crew rises up out of their chairs yelling, protesting, and waving their hands at him.

He just stands there waiting for everyone to say what they have to say. I don't stand up or say anything.

He's got a point—and I guess the State Health and Safety Commission has a point, too.

Our crew has suffered a lot of injuries lately and lost patients we shouldn't have. I see what he means about none of it being our fault, but the rest of the crew doesn't see it that way.

John just stands there taking it all. He doesn't try to make everyone sit down or be quiet.

They go on for at least a minute. This isn't a meeting. It's turning into something more like a civil demonstration.

I'm just starting to wonder when he plans to say something to stop it.

In the middle of the worst commotion, another man walks into the training room. He isn't part of our crew and I've never seen him before.

Dead silence falls over the crew when the guy crosses the room to stop next to John behind the table. Everyone stares at the guy in silent shock.

He's as tall as John and just as muscular, but they look nothing alike.

Rippling burn scars cover the guy's face, head, neck, and most of his arms. He looks like something out of a horror movie.

Brilliant, sea-green eyes blaze out of that haunted face. His nose has melted flat to his face. The burns disfigure his lips and his ears have shrunken way too small. He doesn't have any hair. The burns cover his whole scalp.

He wears the Howe County Fire Department uniform of a tight blue T-shirt, blue pants, and black zip-up boots.

He even wears a black leather belt with a leather multi-tool case on his left side and a paramedic's toolkit on the right.

John raises his hand and grips the man's shoulder through his uniform. I wince when John's fingers squeeze the guy. I expect that touch to hurt the guy's scars, but this man's burns have healed a long time ago.

"This is Carter Holt," John announces. "The State Health and Safety Commission has assigned him to us as our new Health and Safety officer. He's a certified firefighter and paramedic, so he'll be riding along with us and conducting a Health and Safety audit on all our equipment and procedures to make sure we're doing everything possible to protect ourselves and each other."

No one moves or even breathes for a second. None of us can stop staring at Carter.

He just stands there gazing back at us. Our reaction doesn't seem to bother him or make him uncomfortable at all. He must be used to this by now.

Chapter 2: Sophie

A moment of awkward silence falls over the crew as we all stare at Carter Holt. Everyone still stands in the same places they were in when they confronted John.

He finally rallies and says, "If you all want to take your seats, we can get this meeting started."

No one says a word on their way back to their seats. Everyone keeps casting uncomfortable glances at Carter.

I've never seen anyone or anything like this before. Whatever caused those burns must have been awful, but he certainly seems to have recovered well.

If I can somehow block the scars out of my mind, I can see that he's strong, healthy, and takes excellent care of himself. He looks as good from the neck down as any firefighter in this room.

He waits until we all sit down. No one speaks until John turns to him, claps him on the shoulder again, and says, "I'll leave you to it."

John crosses the room and sits down in one of the chairs next to Keith and Danny. John faces front like he's one of the crew about to hear what Carter has to say for the first time.

Carter waits for John to sit down and then faces the room. Carter starts talking in a clear, deep tone that sends shivers up my spine.

He paces back and forth behind the table. We can all see the muscles of his arms, chest, and shoulders through his T-shirt. He commands the room and holds us all spellbound as he begins to speak.

"I know none of you asked for this," he begins. "I worked as a firefighter in Gransworth for seven years before I became a Health and Safety inspector and I've been working as a firefighter and paramedic the whole time I've been doing that—the same way I'm going to be working as a firefighter and a paramedic here. I know how nerve-racking these audits can be—and believe me, I know how annoying it can be to have your Health and Safety officer with you on a call when you're trying to concentrate and you feel like the person is breathing down your neck judging everything you do and say."

A shiver of anxiety goes through the room. He sure called a spade a spade. Everyone in this room is thinking exactly what he just said.

He turns to pace back the other way. "I can also see that you're all unnerved by the way I look. I understand I'm probably not what you were expecting. I never am. I know what I look like and I know I make people uncomfortable. I got caught in a burning house when I was young. Firefighters and paramedics just like you pulled me out and saved my life. I wouldn't be here right now without them. They're the reason I became a firefighter—and they are also the reason I became a Health and Safety inspector. Our job is dangerous enough already. I want to make sure each of you has the best possible working conditions we can give you. You deserve that. I'm here to make sure there are no loopholes or blind spots that could put any of you in more danger than you absolutely have to be."

"No blind spots or loopholes caused some psycho to run Billy over with his car," Caleb blurts out. "No way are you pinning that on any of us."

Carter turns to face him. "No one is pinning anything on anyone. None of this is about blaming any of you for doing anything wrong."

He waves at the stack of files in front of him. They seem to cast such a damning light over the crew. It's a big stack with some of the worst injuries we've suffered since I've been working here.

"Since you bring up Billy's accident......" Carter begins again.

"It wasn't an accident, man," Vince Jaeger cuts in.

"That's my point, isn't it?" Carter opens the file on top of the stack. "Since you bring up Billy's injuries....." He pauses and frowns at Caleb. "Caleb, isn't it? Caleb Watts?"

Caleb squirms in his seat and glances around. "Uh...yeah."

"Since Caleb brings up Billy's injuries, why don't we start with that? We can go over each incident and dissect exactly what happened and where procedures broke down if they broke down at all."

"Nothing broke down," Danny points out. "He was helping a patient. Billy had his back turned when the car broke the Police cordon."

"Exactly! The car broke the Police cordon," Carter replies. "So if there was a failure anywhere along the chain, it must have been with the Police."

He switches on the laptop, scrolls on the device, and brings up a diagram showing the layout of the call where Billy got hit by the car.

Carter points out different places on the diagram in multiple places. "The incident report states that Billy was working on his patient here and that the assailant drove into the scene here. The Police officers responsible for controlling vehicle traffic around the scene were placed here and here. They also positioned squad cars here, here, and here, to block anyone from breaking through to put any of you or the patients in danger."

"Then how do you say the bastard got his car into the scene?" Keith demands.

"The Police sectioned off two of the three highway lanes," Carter explains. "The Police left one lane free so a one-way flow of traffic could pass. The ladder truck was here. The rescue truck was here. The ambulances were positioned here and here. The Police left a space here between the line of traffic and the scene so ambulances could get in and out as soon as they loaded on patients. The assailant got himself into the line of traffic coming from here. He broke onto the scene through that gap and gunned his engines to run down Billy and the two boys."

Another crushing silence falls over the crew when we remember Billy's accident. The incident still casts a chill on all of us.

Carter waits only a minute to let that sink in. Then he brings up a different diagram. It's an expanded view of the same scene from above.

"The Police reports from the vehicular homicide detectives indicate that the assailant struck the victims' car here—more than a mile down the road. Both vehicles were traveling at highway speed. The momentum of the victim's car caused it to flip and then it kept sliding before it hit the retaining wall, flipped again, and crashed. The Police report indicates that the assailant probably stopped there—at a distance from the scene. Then he advanced closer so he could either keep an eye on the victims and-or be within range so he could strike again. That's how he got into the line of traffic so he could be in position to enter the scene when he did."

"Why are you telling us all of this?" Billy interrupts. We can all hear his voice shaking. This must be so hard for him.

Carter pretends not to hear the obvious emotion in his voice. "I'm telling you to explain why an incident like this could happen through no fault of your own. My assessment of this incident is that there was no fault along any of the chain of Health and Safety procedures. Even the Police did everything right. It isn't like they could completely blockade the scene with squad cars and concrete barricades. They had to leave at least one gap for the ambulances to get in and out. That's the vulnerability the assailant used to attack you—and no one could have known he was in that line of traffic. He blended in with all the other vehicles."

His comments don't put the crew at ease at all. "What about the other incidents?" Brooke asks. "Is that what this is about? Do we really have to dredge up the worst incidents of the past few years and go over them with a fine-toothed comb to figure out if any of us did anything wrong?"

"You don't have to," Carter replies. "That's what I'm here for."

Right then, the fire alarm sounds. It blares through the firehouse and startles everyone out of their seats.

Carter looks up at the ceiling, but the tension of this meeting keeps everyone frozen in place. No one reacts right away.

John gets to his feet. "Let's roll, people! Get out there and get to your trucks. Carter will be coming with us to see how we do."

Those words set everyone in motion. They can't get out of the room fast enough. Any disaster will be better than facing Carter and his inspection.

Chapter 3: Carter

I walk out into the Howe Firehouse garage, step into a pair of spare turnouts from the wall by the supply cabinets, and rush over to the rescue truck with the rest of the crew.

I climb into the middle seat, finish sticking on my helmet, and zip up my coat while the other firefighters and paramedics load up with me.

I run through their personnel files in my head while I buckle my seatbelt. Keith Brewer, Fire Chief Brewer's brother, fires up the truck's engines.

Billy Cates sits next to him and switches on the computer to check the dispatch notes. Caleb Watts and Ellis Barrett sit on either side of me in the middle seat.

"What is it this time?" Ellis Barrett yells from my right. He jerks his thumb toward me. "Make it an old lady with a cat stuck in a tree. We don't want anything dangerous for Freddy Kruger here."

"Watch it, chump!" Keith barks over his shoulder. "Show the man some respect."

"It's all right," I tell him. "I'm used to it."

"That doesn't make it okay." Keith glares at Ellis. "Don't let me hear you talking like that again."

"It looks like someone set off the fire alarm at the school," Billy interrupts. "It could be nothing."

"Not likely. Look." One of the female paramedics shoots out her hand and points through the garage door.

The two paramedics in the back are Sophie McNish and Naomi McFee. Sophie is a tall, statuesque, blonde bombshell with crystal blue eyes and magnificent curves.

Fire department uniforms usually make women look blocky and frumpy. Uniforms have a tendency to exaggerate every flaw and indiscretion in a woman's figure.

Sophie's uniform has the opposite effect. It hugs her trim waist, her curved hips, her muscular glutes, and her tight shirt shoves out her full bust so it stands straight out. She looks like something from a Fire Department pin-up calendar.

I have to stop myself from checking her out, so I face front even though she sticks her arm inches away from my face.

Naomi is a small, petite, dark-haired, dark-eyed seductress with witchy olive skin and a sultry kind of charm that would intoxicate anyone.

She doesn't have the quite same effect that Sophie does. She looks like a supermodel even with her hair in a ponytail with a Fire Department baseball cap over her hair.

She has to take her hat off to put on her helmet, but I don't look at that. I don't let myself turn around.

She points down the block where we can all see smoke billowing from the roof of the Howe Elementary School.

"I sure hope the kids are okay," Keith mutters.

Billy reads from the computer. "The notes say all the kids have evacuated the building. Everyone is accounted for."

Keith pulls the truck out onto the street. We only have a few seconds' drive before we get to the scene.

The principal, a few other members of the staff, and a dozen Police officers come out to meet us when the truck pulls into the driveway.

Five Police officers already stand at the school gate to stop concerned parents from entering the premises.

I glance around the rest of the grounds. The teachers and the entire student body crowd onto the basketball courts at a safe distance from the school buildings.

"Are you sure everyone is out of the building?" Chief Brewer asks the principal.

"We did five different head counts," the principal replies. "Everyone is out here. There shouldn't be anyone else in the building."

"What about the maintenance staff?" I ask.

"They're all out here, too—I mean, all the maintenance staff who were scheduled on shift today are all out here."

"Where's the fire coming from?" Chief Brewer asks.

The principal points to the other side of the campus. "The alarm system in the office identified it as the old sports equipment shed by the track field. I can't imagine what could have caught fire there. There's nothing in there but a bunch of old balls, volleyball nets, and soccer goals."

Chief Brewer points at him and then sweeps his arm out toward the basketball courts. "Keep everyone away until we give you the all-clear." He waves the rest of us forward. "Keith, bring the truck around to the track field. The rest of you—let's go."

We file through the school grounds, but we don't enter any of the normal school buildings. They're all perfectly intact. The sports shed is too far away from everything to put the rest of the school in danger.

Chief Brewer could have let the rest of the students and staff return to their classrooms, but he probably just wants to be careful.

He doesn't look at me once, so I have no reason to think he's being extra cautious just because I'm here.

Everyone else seems to have forgotten I'm here—which is a good thing. I don't want them walking on eggshells.

We circle the school building just as Keith drives the truck around. The paramedics and EMTs bring the two ambulances, but the crew leaves the ambulances and the ladder truck parked on the sidewalk outside the school grounds. We can all see we won't need them to transport anyone.

Flames lick off the shed roof and up its side walls. "Get those hoses out!" Keith orders. "Let's put it down so we can all go home."

The crew starts pulling out their hoses. The principal shows me and Ellis where to hook the hoses up to the school's emergency water supply.

Ellis grins at me while we screw off the nozzle cover. He keeps his voice low so Keith won't hear him teasing me. "Be careful you don't get wet. The water might melt you."

"As soon as this call is over, we'll turn the hoses on you and give you your one bath for the decade," I tell him. "It's high time you broke your streak and hosed out all those mushrooms growing in your butt crack."

He winces in mock pain and bursts out laughing. "Oooo! We got a firecracker here."

"I told you I speak the language. If you take a shot at me, you better be ready to take one back."

He laughs again, but this time, Keith hears him. "Quit fooling around over there! Get that water flowing!"

"It's on!" I call back. "Let it rip."

Ellis and I turn the nozzle and Keith, Billy, and Caleb get on the hose to spray down the flames.

They start by raising the stream above the roof and showering the flames in a curtain of water. The three firefighters beat the flames down as far as the roof.

The guys saturate the roof, but it's already blackened to cinders. Then the guys start spraying down the walls. They have to pass the spray back and forth across the walls to suppress the flames.

One of these passes hits the shed door and blows it inward. Smoke and flames billow from inside and the guys shoot water through the door before they move off.

More smoke plumes from the shed's interior once the hose spray isn't there to pound it away anymore. The guys focus on the outer walls.

The smoke coming from the door rises to the ceiling. It keeps pouring through the doorway, but as it keeps rising, it only blocks out the top third of the doorway.

"Holy shit!" I mutter and grab my self-contained breathing apparatus. I scramble to pull the mask over my face before I stick my helmet back on.

"What are you doing?!" Ellis yells at me.

"Someone is in there! Back me up, Ellis!"

"Hey!" he yells. He dodges back and forth between me and trying to get Keith's attention to stop me from going in there. "You're crazy, man!"

I can't listen to anything else. I dive forward and rush the shed door. My mask protects me from breathing all that smoke.

Keith and the others are just coming back for another pass with the hose. I dive under the spray and it showers all over my turnouts as I lunge through the shed door.

I don't take a minute to stop and check who it is trapped in the shed. I should have listened to the principal when he said there was nothing out here that could have set the shed on fire.

Chapter 4: Carter

I fall halfway across the burning shed doorway when I see two outlines of human figures lying huddled under a blanket.

Whoever this is at least had the good sense to get down on the floor and cover themselves for some protection from the flames.

Fire licks all over the blanket. I scramble to my feet, grab the nearest person by the ankles, and drag the person outside. I strip away the blanket and throw it away before I see who the person is.

It's a young kid barely fifteen years old. His clothes are still smoking and his skin is starting to blister, but at least he's all right.

He coughs and wheezes. Black soot surrounds his mouth, nose, and eyes.

The paramedics attack the kid and I charge back into the shed for the second one. I haul him out and pull his blanket off.

Sophie, Naomi, and the other paramedics are already cutting the first kid's clothes off. Neither of these boys can be more than sixteen.

I strip off my SCBA and get to work helping the other paramedics. Josh brings over the burn kit. The kid howls in pain when Josh and I start cutting the second boy's clothes off.

"Check his airway!" Josh tells me. Then he bends over the kid. "What's your name, man?"

The kid is screaming too loudly to say anything. That gives me plenty of opportunity to see into his mouth and even part way down his throat.

"Burns and smoke damage to his mouth and upper airway!" I tell Josh. "I'm putting him on high-flow oxygen. Keep an eye on his vitals."

I put the boy on oxygen and start trying to put in an IV, but he won't keep still. He thrashes so badly that he throws off the burn blanket Josh is trying to put on him.

"Lie still, man!" Josh tells him. "This blanket will ease the pain by keeping the air away from your...."

The kid screams again and tries to fight me off. I can't keep a hold on his arm and the needle at the same time.

I look up and wave Ellis and Vince toward me. "Hold him down! We need to restrain him so we can treat him. You—over there! Bring a backboard, the restraints, and a gurney over here!"

Ellis looks over his shoulder to see who I'm talking to. Ellis is too busy fighting the patient under control to get the stuff himself.

"That's Andy Skinner," he murmurs to me under his breath. "He's one of the paramedics."

"Am I supposed to care who he is? He isn't treating anyone. He can help us."

I try one last time to start the IV. I have to wait for both Ellis and Vince to hold the kid's arm down so I can make the puncture and set the cannula.

The kid starts thrashing again as soon as we let go of him. He even succeeds in pulling off his oxygen mask.

"His heart rate is through the roof!" Josh tells me over the noise. "I can't tell if he's in shock or just agitated."

I glance down at the kid's naked body. "His burns aren't too deep. He's probably just in a lot of pain. Let me give him some morphine." I look up. "Where the hell are those restraints?"

Just then, Chief Brewer walks past watching us. He sees me frowning toward the ambulances. "What's wrong?"

"I just told one of the paramedics to bring the restraints, a backboard, and a gurney over here. He didn't do it and now he's disappeared."

"Who was it?" Chief Brewer asks. "Which paramedic?"

"Andy," Ellis replies over his shoulder.

Chief Brewer purses his lips and storms off to the ambulance. Ellis grins at me. "Put on your crash helmet and get into your nuclear assault bunker."

"That bad, huh?" I ask.

The others laugh. "Andy is.....let's be charitable and say he isn't the most reliable member of our crew."

"That's not good." I have to pay attention to injecting the morphine into my patient's IV.

When I look up the second time, I see Andy and two EMTs coming toward me with the stuff I asked for. Chief Brewer glares at Andy from a distance.

He helps Ellis, Vince, and the others board, restrain, and load up the patient while Josh and I keep working to treat the kid's burns.

He calms down considerably once I dose him up with morphine, but we still restrain him anyway. We strap him down with the burn blanket wrapped around him inside the restraints.

We don't have any trouble keeping an oxygen mask on him, taking his vitals, and monitoring his airway on the way over to the ambulance.

I hand the patient off to Josh and Andy for transport to the hospital. Sophie and the others are already loading up the second patient.

She and Naomi get into the back and drive off. That leaves me and the other firefighters to continue cleaning up the rest of the scene.

Chief Brewer comes over to me while I'm straightening out my SCBA and putting it back in the truck. "That was a great save. You saved those kids' lives."

"You might want to tell the Police to check with the high school," I reply over my shoulder. "Something tells me both boys cut school today."

"What makes you say that?"

"There are paint cans and drug paraphernalia in the shed. That must be how the fire started."

He starts to frown and then relaxes. He clamps his hand on my shoulder the way he did at the firehouse. "I'm really glad you're here. The crew is going to develop a lot more respect for you after today. You won't have any trouble with them anymore."

I purse my lips. I shouldn't say it, but I have to. "You're going to have to do something about Andy. He's letting his attitude put patients in danger."

His features go dark again. "I know, man. I appreciate you saying something. We've been so shorthanded for so long that I like to pretend it isn't happening."

"Have you at least given him a disciplinary warning about it?" I ask.

"I haven't seen him doing anything that would call for that. I know he isn't the most energetic member of our crew, but I haven't seen him doing anything that's blatantly against procedure—not that would warrant a warning or a demotion or anything like that. He just does the bare minimum."

"Well, you better give him one for today. He disobeyed a direct order from a senior firefighter and delayed essential patient care. If that doesn't warrant it, I don't know what does."

His eyes fly open. "He did?"

"Yes! You can ask Josh if you don't believe me. Vince and Ellis were both there, too. The patient was so combative that we couldn't treat him. I told Andy to bring the restraints over. He walked away and didn't come back. What more do you want to know?"

Now it's his turn to purse his lips. "I didn't know that. I didn't know he was interfering with patient care."

"File the warning," I tell him. "If you don't, I'm going to have to include it in your audit. This is exactly the kind of thing I'm here to assess."

He only nods at me. "Of course. You're absolutely right. Thank you for telling me."

He walks away toward his pickup and I go back to helping Keith, Billy, and the others roll up the hoses. The fire is out.

By the time we finish, Chief Brewer tells the principal that the teachers can take the children back inside. Chief Brewer tells us to load up in the truck and go back to the firehouse.

Chapter 5: Sophie

The first thing I see when I jump out of the back of the ambulance is Carter Holt standing in the firehouse garage. Ellis. Vince, Josh, Keith, Danny, Billy, and Caleb surround Carter all talking like the best of friends.

Naomi, Chris, Emily, and I go over to them. "That was freakin' incredible!" Chris exclaims and elbows Josh in the arm. "You better watch out. We got a new Superman on the block."

"Hardly," Carter mumbles.

"How did you see those kids in the shed?" Ellis asks. "I didn't see anything but a whole lot of smoke and flames."

"I saw the outline of their shapes in the flames." Carter looks away. "I guess I'm just extra sensitive to seeing shapes in flames. I used to have nightmares about it after the accident."

"It's your superpower," Keith tells him. "We wouldn't have found those kids until after we put the fire out. By then, it would have been too late."

Carter looks over at me. "What happened to them? Are they okay?"

"They're in the burn unit, but neither of them has anything more than second-degree burns. Their smoke inhalation wasn't too severe, either. They're both going to be fine, thanks to you."

I try to smile at him, but he immediately looks away and focuses on the guys.

"Hey, man," Ellis tells him. "We're having a firehouse barbecue on Saturday at the beach. You should come."

Carter raises his eyebrows—or he would except that he doesn't have eyebrows. He raises the burned, scarred skin above his eyes where his eyebrows should be.

"Really?" he exclaims. "Thank you. I would be honored."

"You're definitely one of the firehouse family after today," Danny tells him.

"Just don't include anything from the barbecue in your report," Billy adds.

"Why? Are you doing dangerous things at the barbecue?" Carter asks. "Tell me you aren't skydiving into the area or holding archery contests with your crewmates as the targets."

The others burst out laughing and Danny elbows Keith. "He got you so bad, bro! Do you hear that? You better warn the old lady!"

Carter looks back and forth between them and all of us. "Did I miss something? I was just joking."

"Keith's wife Leila was a paramedic here before she got pregnant," I tell him. "That was her thing. She was always coming up with whacky ideas to make the barbecues more interesting."

"Like we need them to be more interesting," Billy growls. "We want boring. We want tedious and mundane. The barbecues are supposed to be relaxing, not nightmare-inducing adrenaline-fests."

The others laugh some more. Carter looks even more confused.

"Leila had the idea for us to skydive into the area and to set up targets so we could do archery on the beach," I explain.

"John and Ellen shut her down because there are always so many kids running around," Ellis tells me. "Too dangerous."

"Maybe I *should* do a Health and Safety audit on the barbecues," Carter teases.

The others laugh. "You don't have to because we don't do any of that crap," Billy tells him. "Relaxing, remember? Tedious?"

Carter smiles. His lips don't function the same as a normal person's, but his eyes twinkle with just as much light.

I find myself studying him at close range. He's such a strange combination of ugly and appealing. I can start to see how he's really a normal guy under all those scars.

He doesn't shy away from bantering with the crew. They all accept him, now that we've seen that he's one of us.

Ellis starts making some joke about the Wicked Witch of the West. No one laughs except Carter, but right then, we hear footsteps on the stairs coming down from the firehouse's second level.

Another dangerous silence falls over the group when Andy comes downstairs followed by John.

The rest of the crew disperses without a word. Everyone gets busy doing anything else. Andy shoots us all a death glare and heads off to the training room for some reason.

The other firefighters start working on pulling out their houses, hanging them up to dry, and repacking them into their compartments under the truck.

Naomi and I start restocking our equipment after the call. "What's the problem with Andy?" I ask once we get out of earshot.

"I don't know," she murmurs back. "Maybe one of the guys can tell us."

We find out the whole sordid tale when we go into the drug locker. Josh is in there with Carter. They work together to restock Josh's drug box from the first ambulance.

Carter leaves first. "What's going on with Andy?" Naomi asks Josh. "Did something happen on the call?"

Josh lowers his voice to a murmur. "John hauled him up for disciplinary action for his behavior on that call. Carter gave Andy an order to help us out with our patient. Andy ignored him, walked away, disappeared, and left us swinging in the wind until John went and told him to help us."

"Wow, that's terrible," I exclaim.

Josh glances behind him toward the door to make sure no one can hear him. He lowers his voice even further to a half-whisper. "We don't know for certain, but we think Carter told John to put the screws on Andy for endangering a patient."

"It's about time," Naomi counters. "Andy has always been a slacker. He shouldn't even be on the crew if he lets his attitude interfere with patient care."

They both leave. I'm too busy getting the rest of my supplies, but I can't stop thinking about what Josh just said.

This is the first time in a very long time that John has disciplined anyone on our crew. He never had to before.

I can't decide if I'm happy about Carter stepping in and being the one to tell John to do it now.

We all like to think we're one big happy family. We all like to think John respects us too much to discipline us for anything. We all like to think we're too honorable and professional ever to do anything that would make him discipline us.

If Josh is right, then it's high time someone pulled Andy into line. It's true he's always been a slacker and has always had a bad attitude.

He's also a very good paramedic when he wants to be. He's saved more lives than I can count.

I can't blame Carter for doing his job. He's here to improve Health and Safety for the whole fire crew and all our patients.

If Andy really did ignore a direct order to do something and that disobedience interfered with patient care, then a disciplinary warning is the least that he deserves.

Carter wouldn't be doing his job if he let Andy get away with that. Carter wouldn't be doing his job if he let John get away with letting it slide.

I gather up my stuff and head back to the truck. Carter is standing at the back door talking to Naomi about something. I have to wedge myself in next to Carter to hand the stuff up to Naomi so she can put it in the drug box.

I would normally climb up there to help her do it, but something stops me. I don't feel like I can walk away from Carter in case he has something he wants to tell me about the way I'm doing my job.

I catch him glancing at me while I do my work, but when I face him and try to return eye contact, he immediately looks away again. Is something wrong? Is he thinking about writing me up for something next?

Chapter 6: Sophie

I get out of my car, hoist a giant box out of the back seat, and balance on one foot while I kick the door shut.

I head down to the beach. The fire crew and off-duty friends and family are already gathering down there.

The Brewer brothers hold court over the barbecue as usual. The rest of the adults stand around, drink, shoot the breeze, and help themselves to the food at the picnic table.

A bunch of kids run around screaming on the sand, dive into the waves, and struggle out before they go back to playing with their friends.

I put my box on the table and take out a giant chocolate cake and an enormous tin of cookies.

Ellis shows up just in time to take the tin out of my hand. "Marry me, Sophie," he teases. "I need a woman who knows how to cook for me."

I laugh at him. "You would be too fat to climb into the truck if I cooked for you, you gluttonous pig."

He takes out a cookie, stuffs it into his mouth, and mumbles with his cheeks bulging. "Gluttonous pig. That's the greatest compliment anyone has ever given me."

I snicker on my way back to my car. I'm just lifting a loaded cooler out of the trunk when the rescue truck pulls into the beach parking lot. Everyone else is already here.

Carter pulls in just then driving his own personal pickup. He hops out of the driver's seat and comes over to me. "Let me carry that for you."

I step back and try not to let my cheeks burn too much. "Thank you," I tell him.

He barely looks at me before he lifts the cooler and carries it away down the beach.

His back and shoulders swell up with muscle when he takes the weight. He carries it easily and doesn't look back.

Vince, Josh, Jessie Nash, Andy, and the other firefighters from the ladder truck unload right behind Carter.

Andy shows no sign that he has a problem with Carter coming to the barbecue. Maybe Andy is finally learning to keep his attitude in check after all.

The crew heads down to the beach while I take the last shopping bags out of my car. Jessie hangs back and comes over to me on the way down there.

She's a tiny, wiry, elfish woman with a sense of humor way too big for her body.

"So....?" She juts her chin down toward the beach. "The new Health and Safety officer....."

"What about him?" I ask. "He seems very competent—and he sure knows his way around an emergency scene."

She grins at me. "He's hot! Admit it."

I turn bright red and look away. "I'm sure he would disagree with you."

"Come on!" she chides. "I mean—look at those shoulders. He's gorgeous."

I don't answer. Gorgeous isn't the word I would use for Carter, but he's definitely captivating.

He puts my cooler with the others and then joins the group to start socializing with the crew.

"Hey! Freddy's in the house!" Ellis crows as soon as Carter shows up.

Chris gasps. "Ellis! How could you?"

"He's just expressing his affection," Carter explains. "Don't worry. I went through high school like this. I've heard it all." He turns to Ellis. "So when are you going to enter the biohazard unit for your annual decontamination? I heard an alien strain of slime mold was planning to colonize your armpits as soon as they can invent a life support system strong enough to withstand the noxious gasses."

Everyone explodes with laughter, including Ellis. "I think you've finally met your match, Ellis," Josh tells him. "It's time to hang up your boxing gloves."

"Never." Ellis throws back his shoulders. "I have not yet begun to humiliate myself."

The others keep snickering at both of them.

"Does anyone know what happened to our two high school delinquents?" Danny asked.

"They're still in the burn unit," Ellen tells us. "They did get questioned by the Police, though."

"Here I thought I was a screw-up in high school," Ellis chimes in. "I was downright saintly compared to those two."

"They obviously weren't thinking about the risks," Josh points out. "They were sniffing paint fumes and smoking meth in the same enclosed space."

"They were smart to get under those blankets," Carter adds. "I wish I had thought of that."

His comments cast a chill over the group, but instead of the conversation falling into awkward silence, Chris turns to him. *"Would* it have helped you?"

"I suppose not. I was sound asleep when the fire broke out. The fire consumed enough oxygen in the room that I passed out before I realized what was going on. I didn't wake up until I was in the ambulance on the way to the hospital. Then I wished I hadn't woken up at all."

"It's amazing to meet someone who has gone through it on the other side," I remark. "We don't usually get to talk to the people we pull out of burning houses. We'll probably never get to talk to those boys. It's mind-blowing to actually get to talk to someone who was a patient of another fire crew."

He glances at me once before he looks away again. He doesn't respond in any other way.

His eyes lock onto me for a split second of significant eye contact—almost like he wants to say something else—but he doesn't.

A bunch of kids distract us right then. They all surround their parents all talking at once. A few different adults wander away to get the kids something to eat.

I get pulled into talking to Brooke, Naomi, and Jessie. Jessie starts telling us about the call she and the ladder truck went on right before they came here.

By the time we break up to go in different directions, the rest of the group is standing around talking again.

I spot Carter standing by the picnic table loading up a plate of food. The way he avoids looking at me is starting to make me mad. He better not have a problem with me. He doesn't even know me.

I go over there just as he lifts a slab of cake out of my container. He takes a massive bite before he adds it to his plate.

I laugh at him. "Be careful. The single ladies on our crew won't think you're such a stud if you keep eating like that."

He pretends not to hear the compliment. "This cake is fantastic! Who brought it?"

I hesitate and then blurt out. "I did. I made it."

His eyes snap to my face and he doesn't look away this time. "You made that?! You have to give me the recipe."

I raise my eyebrows. "Recipe? You mean...you cook?"

"I learned in rehab. What did you do to it?" He takes another bite. "This is unbelievable. It tastes like it came from a store."

I blush and look away. "Don't you think you better eat some real food first? Would you like me to get you something?"

He nods at his plate. "I think I have enough—and I wouldn't want Billy to think I was stressing myself out."

I laugh again. He sure is charming. I turn to the table to get something for myself. Right then, his eyes dip to my clothes before he immediately looks away.

Now it's my turn to pretend not to see. Now I understand why he avoids looking at me. He's attracted to me. He's checking me out.

That realization somehow makes it a thousand times more difficult to talk to him. I expect him to make a tactful excuse to go back to the group, but he doesn't. He just keeps standing there.

"Can I get *you* anything?" He jerks his head over his shoulder toward the barbecue. "It might be too dangerous for a damsel like you to go fight the dragons as they crouch over their bloody prey."

My cheeks turn bright red. "Thanks. You're a prince, but I can bat my eyelashes at them better than you can."

He smiles again. His lips don't twist up in the right way, but his eyes crinkle and twinkle in heart-stopping ways. He looks so boyish and fascinating when he smiles.

"So where are you from?" I ask. "You can't be from around here. Most of the crew grew up around here. They would have known you from before."

"No, I'm not from around here."

I wait for him to say something else. He doesn't.

"Where did you work before this?" I ask. "You said you worked on other fire crews before you started with the Health and Safety Commission."

"Yes, I worked in Whitley, Crayton, and Briarbay."

I frown at the names. "Did the fire happen there? Did you work with the firefighters who rescued you?"

"No, the fire happened on the East Coast. I didn't move out here until after I finished high school."

"How old were you when it happened?"

He barely looks at me. "I was thirteen."

I can't stop staring at him. Why does he fascinate me so much? It might be because he looks so different from every other man I've ever met—or it might be something else.

He looks up and sees me staring at his face. He doesn't look away this time. "Are you sure I can't get you something?" he asks. "Do you want something to drink?"

I snap out of my trance when I realize we're standing here staring into each other's eyes. "Um....okay. Thanks. There are some iced teas in that cooler there."

He smiles at me. "Your cooler, right? Did you bring them for your-self?"

He doesn't wait for me to answer. He puts his plate down, goes to get me one of the cans out of the cooler, and brings it back to me.

He holds it out to me and I become strangely aware of the scars covering his arms. They curl around his knuckles, but they don't extend as far as his fingers.

That moment seems to last an eternity. I see our hands moving closer together. He makes much stronger eye contact with me now. Is that because we're alone together?

We aren't alone together, but we might as well be. I can't see or hear anyone else on the beach.

His voice floats out of the ether—almost like he's whispering in my ear from right next to me. "What about you? Where are you from?"

"I was born and raised in Hamilton. I lived there all my life until I moved up to Howe." I blush again for no reason. "It must sound awfully boring—only living in two places for my whole life."

"It doesn't sound boring at all," he tells me. "Did you always want to be a paramedic?"

"No, I wanted to be a doctor when I was younger."

His eyes drill into me with unnerving power. "So what changed?"

I shrug it off. "I don't know. I started high school and I didn't have many friends. I kind of lost my way and I didn't pull it together until too late in high school. By then, my grades weren't good enough to get into a decent college and I didn't want to go into medicine anymore anyway—not that kind, at least."

He won't stop staring at me. I can't understand why. "That sounds hard," he murmurs.

I try to make a joke out of it. "Not as hard as you had it, I'm sure."

He cocks his head to study me. Is it possible I'm as interesting to him as he is to me? I don't see how I can be. My life is nothing to write home about.

I try to brush it away. "Anyway, I thought I might become a nurse, but then my older brother got into a car accident and I got interested in the paramedics who helped him at the scene. It all went from there and I decided I wanted to do that."

"That's interesting......So is your brother okay?"

"No, he died in the hospital three days later."

His features go hard. "I'm sorry to hear that."

I shrug and tear my gaze away. His eyes leave me nowhere to hide. "I thought losing him would send me into another spiral, but it actually brought me out of the spiral that started before that. Getting interested in emergency medicine helped me through it."

He inclines his head to one side again. "Did you actually spiral? You made it sound like you were just lonely."

"I was both. I had really good friends when I was growing up....and then things fell apart when I got to high school. I lost my best friend....." I choke on the words and try to shake the memory out of my head. "You don't want to hear about all that."

"I do," he breathes. "I want to hear about it."

"I made friends with this boy in kindergarten. His name was Dylan. We lived next door to each other and we used to play in one of our two backyards every day all the way through elementary school and middle school. We spent our last summer together making a bunch of plans for high school. We both knew it was going to be a much bigger challenge. We decided we would always stick together and help each other in case neither of us could make other friends. We got the school to put us in the same class and everything so we would always have someone we trusted in our corner." I break off. "Sorry. I haven't talked about this in years."

"So what happened? Did he die, too?"

"No, he moved away in the middle of the year and I never saw him again. We invested so much in supporting each other that I didn't really know how to cope without him. That's when things started going downhill."

"I'm really sorry you had to go through that." His eyes dip to my body again, but only for a split second. "You seem to have pulled yourself out of it just fine. You look great—and I'm sorry about your brother. That must have been terrible."

I wave that away. "Listen to me feeling sorry for myself talking to someone like you. I have a great life. You don't want to hear about all my tiny little problems."

Chapter 7: Sophie

Jessie and Ellis come over to the picnic table while Carter and I are still standing there. "When are you going to teach Jessie how to cook?" Ellis asks me. "She needs lessons."

"You aren't going around propositioning every single girl on the crew to marry you and become your domestic slave, are you?" I turn to Jessie. "Be careful of this one. He's dangerous."

She laughs at me and then smirks at Carter. "You better be careful, Carter. You might have to include that cake in your Health and Safety report as a health hazard."

He picks up his piece and takes another bite. "I definitely plan to include it. This stuff is criminal."

I find myself laughing, but right then, Keith calls over from the barbecue. "Hey—Carter! What are you eating? We have fried Tyrannosaurus Rex, Stegosaurus steaks, or you can have a Brontosaurus burger."

Carter laughs and crosses to the barbecue. Jessie and Ellis joke around with each other and then leave. That gives me all the time in the world to get my own food.

I don't feel like going back to the group. All that talk about my past puts me in a gloomy mood. It shouldn't. It happened so long ago.

I sit down to eat at the picnic table while I wait for the clouds to pass. They always do.

A few minutes later, Leila comes over and sits down next to me holding little baby Leon. She pulls up her shirt and starts breastfeeding him where I can see them together.

I find myself grinning at them. "Look at the little guy squirming around like a worm on a hook," I tease. "He's gorgeous."

She makes a face. "You can say that because he doesn't keep you up all night with his constant demands. Talk to me in eighteen years about how gorgeous he is."

I laugh. "You're in the trenches now."

She smirks at me. "Thanks. How are you doing? You look good."

I blush and look away when I remember Carter saying that. I don't want him to find me attractive.

He's the firehouse Health and Safety officer. He won't stay around Howe for long. He'll file his audit and then move on to the next firehouse he's supposed to assess.

Looking away from Leila brings me face to face with the group again. They all stand around talking and eating.

Carter joins right in with their conversation. No one would ever think he belonged anywhere else. He blends right in even though he looks so different.

Right then, the minute I look up, he breaks away from the group, walks back to the parking lot, takes a surfboard out of his truck bed, and comes back with it, a black nylon bag, and a towel.

He puts the bag on the ground and sticks his surfboard into the sand by its tail.

"What are you doing?" Billy asks.

"I'm going surfing," Carter replies. "Hold my beer."

"You aren't drinking beer," Ellis points out.

Carter doesn't answer. The whole crew falls silent when he pulls off his shirt, drops it on top of the bag, kicks off his shoes, and starts unbuckling his belt.

He strips off his pants to reveal that he's wearing surf shorts underneath them. He folds all his clothes on top of the bag and starts pulling open the Velcro ankle strap attached to his surfboard leash.

We all sit and stand in silence watching him. Burn scars cover his back, shoulders, and half of his chest.

The burns end at his sternum, flow all the way down his back, disappear under his shorts, and come back out on the backs of his legs. The scars extend all the way down to the middle of his calves.

The skin of his stomach and the fronts of his thighs is normal human skin with an arrow of black hair going down his stomach to his waistband.

He looks even bigger with his shirt off. Every ripple of muscle shows up under his scars when he folds his clothes and bends over to strap the Velcro around his ankle.

No one even tries to hide that we're all staring at him in amazement. This is the first time anyone at any of the firehouse barbecues has ever even thought to go surfing.

Leila didn't think of it, either, for some reason. She thought of every other activity we could be doing, but not that.

He pretends not to notice us staring at him. He pulls his surfboard out of the sand and we all gape at him in slack-jawed shock when he walks down the sand to the water's edge.

The kids pause their game to watch, too, but they go back to what they were doing when he starts striding into the waves.

He wades up to his waist before he dives on top of his board and starts stroking out into the deep water.

Swimming like that makes his back and shoulders look even broader and more muscular. His scars accentuate the movement of each muscle under the skin. He really is captivating.

In a minute, he makes it out beyond the breaker zone, finds the place he wants, and sits up to straddle his board to wait.

The others go back to what they were doing. People lose interest in Carter, but I can't. I keep watching until he sees a promising wave, turns his board around, starts paddling, and catches it.

He surfs to the shore before he drops off. He comes up blowing water out of his nose and mouth. Then he shakes his head sideways to get the water out of his ears.

He jumps onto his board and starts paddling out there to do it all again.

A few people come over to the picnic table and I realize I shouldn't be staring at a guy I don't even know.

I stand up, go over to the group, and talk to my friends and coworkers for a while, but I can't get interested in whatever they're talking about.

Carter is still out there. It's amazing that he can do so much and that he's fully embraced who and what he is despite what he's been through.

I get a sense again that he represents all the patients we never get to find out about. How many burn victims have I treated between the scene and the hospital?

I never see them again. I don't see how they survive after the fact, what they look like, or how they cope with their injuries.

Seeing Carter like this gives me new energy to keep doing this work. Some unknown paramedics saved him.

I might have given some of my patients another chance like that. I might have inspired someone the way those unknown paramedics inspired him. It's pretty amazing to think about.

I see now why he decided to become a Health and Safety officer. He represents everything good and noble about this job. He's a living breathing example of why we all chose this line of work.

He eventually gets tired of surfing, swims to shore, and all the kids surround him when he walks out dripping onto the sand.

He talks to them and then turns around to point and explain things to them about the waves out there.

I'm not the only one who breaks off the conversation to watch him. No one comments when he comes back over to us, jams his surfboard tail downward into the sand, and starts drying himself off with his towel.

He eventually takes his stuff back to his truck, puts his surfboard in the bed, and changes his clothes in the cab. He comes back down to the group fully dressed and the whole barbecue goes on as before.

He gets swept into the conversation about work and life in Howe and he gets to know everyone else here.

No one says anything to him about it, but I hear so much in that reverent silence and even the soft murmurs of the few people who do keep talking.

Everyone here realizes who and what this person is to us now. He's one of us, but he's so much more than that. He's an inspiration.

Chapter 8: Carter

I flip a page in one of the firehouse procedure manuals, bend over one of the rescue truck's outer storage compartments, and check the hinge where the door is supposed to swing open.

I unlatch the door, lift it, and it swings upward. I have to squat down to get the tools out of it.

I put the door down and rummage through the manual again. I hunt around the specifications for the door and the truck's maintenance logs.

I'm just flipping back to the specifications and frowning to myself when Sophie comes around the back of the truck.

Everyone else on the crew is upstairs in the breakroom. I thought I was the only one down here. That's why I chose now to perform this inspection. I don't want to make the crew nervous.

She doesn't come from the stairs. She comes from the other side of the garage.

She waltzes right up to me. "Are you busy right now?" she asks even though she can see that I am.

"No," I reply. "What can I do for you?"

"Would you mind coming over to the second ambulance? I want to ask you something."

She shouldn't be asking me anything about the ambulance. She should be asking Chief Brewer if she has any questions or concerns. Then he would be the one to raise it with me.

I would have heard about that if she did bring something up with him. I try not to stiffen when I realize she's making an excuse to talk to me.

I can't let myself get involved with her. For a start, I'm her superior here and I won't be staying at Howe for very long.

She must know that, so why is she making it so obvious that she's interested in me?

I don't put the manual down when I follow her over to the ambulance. She leads me to the back and climbs inside.

I make a strategic decision to stand outside. Getting into the back of an ambulance with her would put both of us in a compromising position, especially when we're alone together.

She pulls out the nebulizer from under the bench seat, pops open the machine's protective box, and shows me the device inside.

"Do you see this prong here where the rechargeable battery fits into the slot?" She points to the back of the unit. "See how this prong is at an angle from the others? It was always straight before. I just noticed that it's bent—but the unit just came back from a maintenance check. The person who checked it must have missed this."

"No, it's supposed to be like that. See? Look at this." I flip a few more pages in my procedure manual. "The unit went in for maintenance four weeks ago and the technician straightened the prong." I turn to a different page. "The specs list the angle it's supposed to be, so it would have been off before when you saw it straight. The technician corrected it. It's supposed to be like this."

"Oh." She frowns at the unit and then at me. "Are you sure? It's never been bent like that before in all the time I've been working here."

I stare back at her. Is she really asking me if I'm sure about something safety-related? "Was there something else you wanted?"

She opens her mouth, but no sound comes out. I become aware of her staring at me the way she did at the beach.

I should get back to my inspection, but I can't bring myself to just walk away from her. God, she's beautiful!

She glances down at the unit in her hands and flounders for something to say.

"Thank you for bringing it up," I offer. "It's good to know that everyone on the crew is keeping an eye open for these things."

Just then, the crew comes downstairs for some reason. Jessie joins us, climbs into the back of the ambulance, and she and Sophie start talking about some other equipment and supplies that Chief Brewer needs to replace.

I take the opportunity to escape back to my inspection of the rescue truck. I make a note of the cabinet door and move on to the hoses themselves.

A few minutes later, Chris, Josh, Danny, and Naomi happen to wander closer to the truck and see what I'm doing. "Are the gremlins at it again, Sherlock?" Danny teases.

I don't take the joke. I flip to the maintenance schedule instead. "This says you haven't replaced your hoses in over seven years."

They exchange glances. "Should we have?" Josh asks.

Just then, Jessie and Sophie walk around the truck from the other side, see us, and come over to join us. At least now I can pretend that Sophie isn't here. She won't do anything inappropriate in front of the crew—not that she's ever done anything inappropriate before.

Why am I worried about that—apart from the irresistible temptation to do something inappropriate with her? I really need to stop thinking about that.

The rest of the crew works on their vehicles or organizes the supply cabinets across the garage. The noise fills the area with a kind of peaceful music. The tension of our first meeting dissolves. My presence doesn't bother anyone anymore.

Keith, Billy, and Andy come over next. Keith nods at the manual in my hands. "Are you finding anything incriminating?"

"Incriminating—no," I reply. "I am finding things that need to be fixed or changed."

"Like what?" Billy asks.

"See this cabinet?" I point the locker on the side of the truck. "The door swings upward. It's supposed to swing downward. If it swings upward, it poses a risk of either falling on someone's hands or head when they try to get the tools out or of someone hitting their head or shins on it."

"But the truck has already gone in for maintenance multiple times," Sophie points out. "The mechanics should have corrected that.....Sh ouldn't they?"

"Yes, they should have—but the problem is that you're operating with an outdated procedures manual. There's nothing in the maintenance checklist to check for that or correct it if it's found to be opening the wrong way."

"So what are supposed to do about that?" Keith asks. "John would be the one to get updated manuals, wouldn't he?"

I flip a few more pages in the manual, but I can already see that this inspection is a waste of time. "The strangest part is that the State Health and Safety Commission is the body responsible for keeping all your policy and procedure manuals up to date—and for keeping all the maintenance crews' policy and procedure manuals up to date. If someone is falling down on the job, it's the Commission."

Jessie bursts out laughing. "You better take it to the top, Jefferson. You're the only one here with the firepower to take on the commission."

"I will." I shut my manual and turn to the rest of the crew.

I plan to make some quippy remark, but I don't seem to be able to do that with Sophie standing right there.

Her presence dominates my awareness. Her presence blasts into me from just a few feet away.

I shouldn't let her affect me this much, but she does. Am I that desperate that I'll let myself get distracted by a woman just because she's interested in me?

I'm interested in her, too. That's the terrible truth. I was interested in her before we started talking on the beach. She hypnotizes me. I find it hard to think straight when she's around.

I barely hear the others' conversation. I only listen enough to know they aren't talking about anything firehouse-related. Then I make a dignified exit by going back up the Chief Brewer's office.

He's on the phone and doesn't get off when I go in there to put the manual away. I head for the breakroom to work on my report. The rest of the crew is downstairs. I can sit by myself and think.

This audit is turning out to be a completely different animal than anything I've ever done before. Then again, Howe Firehouse is like no place I've ever worked before.

Everyone here sticks up for each other. They're all amazingly close and defensively protective of each other and their firehouse.

I've never met a crew that cares so much about doing a good job and taking care of each other.

The way they've welcomed me into their little family is really touching. I can understand why and how a fire crew closes ranks when they realize they're under inspection for something like this.

No crew has ever opened its arms to me like this. No other crew has ever invited me to their private social functions or made me feel so at ease.

I've also never seen a firehouse as well-run as this one. I can find a lot of things wrong with it, but I can't trace any of those back to human error on the crew's part or Chief Brewer's mismanagement.

These people really know their stuff—and why shouldn't they? They all dedicate themselves to the job and they make sure to do it right.

I come out of Chief Brewer's office with my head somewhere completely different. I'm just about to walk into the breakroom when Andy comes around the corner from the stairs.

He must have followed me up here and I see right away that he came here to confront me.

His mouth hardens and he narrows his eyes when he pulls up in front of me. "I got something to say to you, man," he growls.

I only nod. "Say it, then."

"You got me written up," he blurts out. "Now I have a disciplinary reprimand on my permanent record. It's the first one in my entire career. I was doing just fine before you came along and started sticking your nose into everything."

I wait for him to say something else. "Is that it?" I ask. "Is that all you wanted to say—because I already know that I got you written up and I already know that Chief Brewer gave you a disciplinary reprimand on your permanent record. What about it?"

"So—what do you have to say for yourself?" he demands. "You don't even know me and you think you can walk in here and screw up my life for no reason!"

I pretend to raise my eyebrows. "For no reason? You think putting a critical patient in danger because you have a stick up your ass is no reason?"

"I did not put a patient in danger...!" he blusters.

"I told you point blank to bring the restraints over. I know you heard me and I know you saw us struggling to restrain the patient. We couldn't treat him because it took all four of us just to hold him down. You didn't bring the restraints. You walked away and you didn't come back. Were you aware that I'm superior in rank to everyone here—including Chief Brewer? Were you aware of that?"

He compresses his lips. "So? What does that have to do with anything? You're a paramedic and I'm a paramedic. We're the same rank."

"Not in this capacity—and you just admitted that you *did* know I was superior in rank. You brought the restraints when Chief Brewer told you to but you chose to ignore me. You deliberately put that patient in danger. Why? Do you have a problem with me? You better say so right now. If you can give any reason why you acted like that, you better tell me right now."

He hesitates and then points in my face. "You keep away from Sophie. Do you hear me? I see what you're doing. You keep away from her."

I stare at him in stupid shock. "Sophie! What does she have to do with this?" I think fast. "I never even had a conversation with her before that call."

"Sophie and I....." He breaks off and corrects himself. "You just keep away from here. It's bad enough that you come in here and start throwing your weight around. You keep away from what doesn't belong to you. Understand?"

He turns on his heel to walk away. I lunge forward to grab his arm. "I heard what you said. Now you're going to hear what I have to say. I have no intentions at all toward Sophie and I have never done anything to indicate to her, to you, or to anyone else on the crew that I did have intentions toward her—but let me tell you one thing right now, man. If it was up to me, you would be out on your ass with no chance to work in the emergency field anywhere ever again. Do I make myself clear? If I was in charge of this firehouse, you wouldn't be getting away with just a disciplinary reprimand—and I would bet cold hard cash that you've done something like this before—probably many times. You got lucky because Chief Brewer considers you a part of the firehouse family—but there is no way in hell that this was the first time you let your attitude interfere with patient care—or with the functioning of this firehouse—or with your crewmates' safety. I don't know when or where or how you did it, but I know you did it—and I'll be watching you from now on. Chief Brewer might be too nice to say this to you, so make sure you hear it from me. The next time you screw up, you're out. You won't get a second warning. Understand? You better conduct yourself in a perfectly professional manner from now on and start behaving by the book or things will not go well for you."

He glares at me and then turns on his heel and storms off toward the stairs.

I wait until he's out of earshot. Then I inhale a shaky breath and turn into the breakroom.

Now I can definitely put Sophie out of my mind. This is all the more reason why I should give her a wide berth. She and Andy must be a thing.

Chapter 9: Sophie

I take my backpack out of my locker, shut it, and head out to leave the firehouse for the day.

I get a stomach full of butterflies when I see Carter leaving at the same time.

I burst into a smile when I see him. I shouldn't get so excited over someone I'm working with—especially someone of so much higher rank than I am.

It isn't like anything can happen between us. He won't even stick around the firehouse for long. He'll leave soon and I'll never see him again.

He's already walking out of the garage when Andy walks into the locker room and blocks my way. "Can I talk to you for a sec?" he asks.

I stiffen immediately. "No, you can't. Get out of my way."

"Just give me a second. That's all I ask. You owe me that much."

"I don't owe you squat," I fire back. "What the hell do you want?"

He dodges around me, takes my elbow, and pulls me back into the locker room. Everyone is gone. We're alone here.

Just for a second, I wonder if I should just run for it. I don't want to get caught anywhere alone with him.

He would have to be truly deranged to attack a fellow paramedic on firehouse property. I satisfy myself by retreating to arm's length.

He's never acted violently toward me before, but there's a first time for everything.

He's a dyed-in-the-wool prick. That's the one thing I can say about Andy Skinner.

Everyone knows it. He's the asshole of the firehouse. He doesn't care about anyone but himself.

He pretends not to notice me holding him at a distance. "I see the way you're acting around Carter," he begins. "Don't think I don't see what you're doing."

I stare at him and open my mouth to say that I'm not doing anything with Carter. I'm not doing anything with Carter. I've only ever talked to him.

He's been over-the-top polite to me and he was unbelievably attentive and considerate when I told him about my past.

I've never told anyone at the firehouse about any of that. No one has ever asked enough to find out.

Something about Carter makes me trust him. I already know he's caring, gentle, and dedicated to the job. He's everything Andy is not.

I discard the idea of lying about it. "I don't know what you're talking about," I tell him. "But it's none of your business who I get with and who I don't get with. You and I are long over. You have no business even noticing who I get with."

He points at me. "I knew it! You're flaunting it right in front of me! How could you betray me like this?!"

"Betray you! We're done! We haven't gone out in years! Where have you been? You've been out there sleeping with God knows who ever since we broke up. Don't lie about it! I've seen you hitting on girls at bars and going home with them!"

He changes his expression immediately and takes a step toward me. "None of them meant anything to me. We can work this out. I only want us to get back together...."

I shoot out both hands and push him away. "Are you insane?! I would never get back together with you. Do you honestly think I care if you're out there sleeping with half the state? Go right ahead. I don't want you. You're nothing to me. Leave me alone!"

His features turn to granite again. "So you can go run off with Carter?! I'm only saying this because I care about you...."

"You don't give a shit about me. We aren't together and we never will be again. Get that through your head—and just in case, you can say it again for the microphones." I point up at the firehouse security cameras. "If you come near me again, I'll get you reprimanded for sexual harassment."

I grab my backpack and storm out of the locker room. I've wasted enough time on this already.

That dope actually thinks I would get back together with him after our disastrous excuse for a relationship.

I struggle to smile and say goodbye to the rest of the crew in the garage. I make it out to the parking lot behind the firehouse without breaking anything even though I want to.

I pause outside to catch my breath. Andy is so far into my past that I don't even have to think about him.

I shake it off, but when I get out to the parking lot, I see Carter about to get into his truck.

I throw caution to the wind. Andy already thinks I'm hitting on Carter—or the other way around.

Why shouldn't I? Carter is a great guy—one of the nicest I've met in a long time.

I walk right up to him and find myself grinning again just from being near him. "Hey! Do you have plans for tonight?"

He barely glances at me. Are we back to that? "No, I don't have any plans tonight. Do you?"

"Some of us were going out for a few drinks," I tell him. "Do you want to come?"

He looks up and meets my gaze for the first time—and he doesn't look away. He has a way of looking straight into me.

When he answers, he keeps his tone soft and gentle—not challenging or demanding. "Are you inviting me on behalf of the crew—or are you asking me out?"

I turn bright red and wind up laughing and blushing. "Would it be so bad if I asked you out? I like you—a lot. Maybe you could tell."

I try to laugh it off again, but he doesn't even smile. "I don't think that's a good idea," he murmurs. "I'm flattered, but I don't think so."

My laughter dies in an instant. "Can I ask why not?" I take a split second to hesitate before I blurt out the truth. "Is it because of the way you look or because of your job?"

"Does it really matter why?" he asks in the same gentle undertone.

"Yes, it does. If you aren't interested, just say so. I'm old enough to hear the truth."

He opens his mouth to say something and then changes his mind. "It's because you're involved with someone else. Isn't that reason enough?"

My jaw drops and I gasp out loud. I'm just about to ask who the hell I'm supposedly involved with.

Like something out of a bad dream, the rest of the crew comes out to the parking lot right then. I hear Andy talking and joking around with Vince, Theo, and the others.

"It's because of Andy, isn't it?" I growl under my breath. "We aren't together. We haven't been for years. I don't know what he told you...."

Carter raises both hands. "It's none of my business. I'm just passing through here—and I am your senior. It's impossible. I'm sorry."

I do my best not to give him a dirty look before I turn on my heel, but I don't go to my car to leave. I storm up to Andy who is in the middle of goofing around with his friends.

I raise my voice so everyone in the whole crew can hear me. "Do you all want to know why Andy and I split up? That was over four years ago, but he's still out there telling people that we're together to stop me from going out with anyone else. I kept the details to myself because I didn't want to air our dirty laundry in front of the whole crew. Now I have no choice."

No one answers. Silence falls over the parking lot.

Carter stands next to his truck listening. I don't know if this will make any difference, but at least it will stop Andy from shooting off his mouth to anyone else about us being still together.

I point at him. "This slimeball—if I can even insult slimeballs by calling him that—acted like a righteous prick through our whole relationship—just like he acts like a righteous prick with everyone else. He tried to control me, threatened me to stop me from visiting my family, and even tried to blackmail me with videos of us doing it if I didn't do things his way. Then I caught him banging some cocktail waitress in the men's bathroom of a bar downtown and he had the nerve to blame me for not being enough for him. That's how we broke up—so if anyone here ever wonders whether we could ever get back together—we won't. Whatever you may hear to the contrary, I will never get back together with him. I hope I never have to see him again. I only put up with his bullshit when I come here every day because I care about all of you guys and the job so much."

I can't say anything else, so I barge off to my car, get in, turn the motor, and skid out of the parking lot. I can't even look at Carter to see his reaction.

I already know what it will be. My outburst won't change anything because he's right. He is my senior and he won't stay here. It's impossible and I'm the fool for even trying.

Chapter 10: Sophie

I come out of the grocery store, load my groceries into my car, get behind the wheel, and drive home the way I do every time I have a day off.

I go through the same routine of putting my groceries away, doing my laundry, and cleaning my apartment. I have to get everything done on my days off because, once I go back on shift at the firehouse, I won't be able to do anything.

Even in the in-between times when I'm not on shift, I'm too exhausted physically and mentally. I can't do anything but collapse. I don't want to think about anything then.

I even spend time on my days off making a bunch of food ahead of time. I portion it into the freezer so I can grab it and go.

That way I don't have to worry about cooking when I come home after a twenty-three-hour shift of untangling maimed bodies from wrecked cars on the highway.

I can just stick something in the microwave, eat it, and pass out in bed until my next shift.

I also take these microwave meals to the firehouse to eat during my shifts. Then I can eat healthy without doing any extra work.

I finish everything by four o'clock in the afternoon. I have the rest of the day and all day tomorrow to just relax, kick back, and enjoy my life.

I go out into town for a while and browse in a bookstore. I see a lot of books I'd like to read, but I don't usually have time to read anything anyway. I usually get interrupted by firehouse calls just when I'm sitting down to enjoy a really good chapter.

I decide to go to a park and walk around in nature for a while. I take my camera and journal, too, just for fun.

I park at the curb and walk out to the flower garden. I take a bunch of pictures of flowers and the koi fish in the pond.

Then I sits down on the bench next to the pond and write about nothing much while I watch the ducks.

I come to the end of the page and look up to stare off into space while I think about what to write next. Staring off into space is one of my favorite activities to do when I'm not working at the firehouse.

I'm just about to look down to start writing again when some people turn a corner in the park ahead.

The first people in the group are two families with young children making an enormous noise. The kids run around, shriek, point at everything, and fill the park with their shrill voices.

I smile at them for a while. The parents act a lot more disturbed by the noise than I am.

I'm just about to start writing for the second time when another person comes around the corner behind the two families. I freeze when I recognize Carter. It's kind of hard to miss him.

He looks as outstanding as ever in a pair of nice jeans and a blue button-up shirt over a white T-shirt underneath.

He somehow looks bigger in casual clothes—and much more attractive.

He sees me right away. I can't read his expression from here to see if he's stiffening, too. This is just great. The guy has been working at our firehouse for less than two days and I've already made our working relationship uncomfortable by asking him out.

The two families overreact to his presence. The parents make a big deal about getting out of his way. They leave way too much space for him to pass so he doesn't come near them.

Some of the children scream in terror at his appearance. They run to their parents and hold onto their legs in trembling fear.

Some of the kids burst into tears and point at him while they babble incoherently about the monster. Their parents pick them up and comfort them until he passes them.

I cringe at the sight. Poor guy. This must happen a lot.

He's such an awesome guy, too. These foolish people will never know how great he is because they'll never get to know him. What a tragedy—mostly for him.

He barely acknowledges the parents or the kids. His eyes only flicker at them before he goes back to facing front—at least, it probably appears to them that he's facing front.

His eyes go hard and they don't leave my face again. I bend over my notebook. I'm sure he doesn't want to talk to me after I asked him out and after that scene I made with Andy in front of the whole crew.

I'm prepared to go back to my writing and let him walk past me without a word, but without warning, he turns off and sit down on the bench next to me.

"Hi," he murmurs.

"Hi," I mumble back. I don't know what to say to the guy, but I can't just sit here in silence. I look up and immediately feel myself blushing again. "I'm really sorry about yesterday—about all of it. You were absolutely right. It was way out of line for me to ask you out when you're my senior officer and everything—and I'm really sorry you had to hear and see that whole thing with Andy. I'm sorry you got caught in the middle of that."

"It's all right," he murmurs in the same gentle undertone. "I'm really flattered that you asked me out." He pauses for just a split second. "You're the first girl who has asked me out since the accident."

My head shoots up and I find myself gaping at him. "I am? I can't be! I mean...you're so...."

He inclines his head on one side. "I'm what?"

"You're awesome! You're....you're hot! You're....like.......such a stud!"

He barely smiles. He turns away and goes back to looking at the flowers. "You're the only one who thinks so."

"No, I'm not! Even Jessie said so!"

He raises his eyebrows at me. "She did?"

"Of course! She said so at the barbecue. Are you kidding me? Look at you! The way you went surfing like that....and....well...everything. You were an absolute boss on that call at the school.....and on every other call. No one can stop talking about you. Don't you realize how taken everyone is with you? Any girl would be lucky to go out with you. I know it can never happen between us, but...." I stop in mid-sentence and blink at him. "You really don't know, do you?"

"I don't know what?"

"How attractive you are. You think....." The truth hits home. "You think you're ugly, don't you?"

"I am ugly," he murmurs. "Didn't you see the way those people acted just now?"

"You can't take that to mean anything. They're just little kids! They don't know any better."

"Adults act like that, too. Grown men and women act like that. Do you know not one person at any firehouse I've ever worked with has ever asked me to join them for any social gathering—not even a barbecue like that one we had last weekend?"

My jaw drops. "You're kidding!"

He shakes his head. Jesus, he looks so sad—and who could blame him? "They go out together. I hear them talking about it, but they don't ask me."

"Is that because you're their Health and Safety Officer?"

"No, it happened before that when I was just an ordinary firefighter-paramedic. They avoided me."

Now it's my turn to look away. "My God! I am so sorry!"

He looks at me again. His eyes search my soul for something I can't even define for myself.

Maybe hearing that someone thinks he's attractive is so foreign to him that he has to take a minute to accept that I'm telling the truth.

Holy crap! Someone has to tell him. He can't go through life thinking he's the Elephant Man or something.

He deserves a good woman who appreciates him. I know it can't be me, but he deserves someone—someone really good for him.

He stares at me for so long that I start to get uncomfortable. He has an unnerving way of seeing more about me than I might want him to.

"What?" I ask. "I'm telling the truth. You can ask the other women at the barbecue. They'll tell you the same thing."

He doesn't seem to hear me. "I really appreciate what you told me at the barbecue—about how things were for you in high school....."

I grimace and look away. "Please don't think I'm feeling sorry for myself. I got where I need to be. I just had to take a different road to get here—and maybe it was meant to be."

"What do you mean?"

"I don't know. Maybe things wouldn't have worked out between me and Dylan anyway. You know how it is when you get to high school. It wouldn't have worked for a boy and a girl to be best friends. We would have gotten involved with other people or one of us would have started liking the other one and would have gotten their heart broken or something like that. Our friendship probably wouldn't have survived."

"Have you dated anyone since Andy?"

I cringe again. "No. I don't know if I want to date anyone else. I mean—I obviously don't have very good judgment when it comes to men."

"What makes you say that—apart from Andy?"

"Well, I asked *you* out. That was obviously pretty poor judgment."

"Have you made bad choices apart from those two?"

"No," I snap. "I haven't dated anyone besides Andy."

His eyes pop wide open. "You've only dated one person since....since forever?"

"Don't tell anybody," I mutter. "It's embarrassing enough."

"Why?" he asks. "Why haven't you dated anyone?"

I try to shrug it away. "I guess....after Dylan left....I had a really hard time trusting anyone. I trusted him more than anything. It never crossed my mind that I wouldn't always have him there to lean on....."

"Do you think he betrayed you by moving away?"

"No, no. Nothing like that. I never blamed him. I just....I just never met anyone I trusted as much as that. I never met any boys in high school that I even came close to trusting that much. I didn't even trust Andy at the beginning—and I was right."

"Why did you go out with him, then?"

"I only went out with him because I thought I was supposed to. I didn't want to die a virgin and a lonely old cat lady—which is what

I probably will do—I mean, apart from the virgin thing. I did it with him—mainly just to say that I had at least done it with someone. I regret that now. I would rather die a virgin living alone with my cats than have done it with him."

He looks away. This must be making him uncomfortable.

"Sorry," I mumble. "I shouldn't be telling you this."

"No," he murmurs under his breath. "I like talking to you."

My head snaps around, but he doesn't look at me. What is he thinking about right now?

"What about you? Are you really telling me no girl will go near you....just because of the way you look?"

He shakes his head. "I haven't been with anyone. I was just a kid when this happened. People have a pretty strong reaction when they see me—especially women. Just about any guy, no matter how ugly he is, looks better to them than I do. I just try to enjoy my life the way it is. I guess that kind of thing isn't on the cards for me."

"No!" I exclaim. "You'll find someone! I'm certain of it. If it doesn't happen here, it will happen somewhere else. Someone will see you and get to know you. You have your whole life in front of you."

"I loved a girl once....." He trails off. "But it didn't work out."

I brighten up. "Really? Was that after the accident?"

He turns to me. His eyes make me tremble. "Sophie....." He barely breathes.

I gulp. What is he about to say?

He swallows hard and then says in a breathless undertone. "I'm Dylan, Sophie. I'm Dylan McNulty. I lived next door to you back then. I'm really sorry I didn't tell you....."

Chapter 11: Sophie

I gape at Carter with my jaw on the sidewalk. "You're......" I can't breathe for a second. I wouldn't have been able to recognize him—not without all those burns.

My mind goes into a tailspin. I barely hear him. Dylan. Dylan McNulty. Carter Holt is Dylan McNulty—my long-lost best friend.

"I didn't move away, Sophie," he murmurs. "I went to visit my grandmother for Thanksgiving weekend. Do you remember? My parents decided to have Thanksgiving at our house—and then they got a phone call on Wednesday night that my great-uncle was coming home from overseas to have dinner with my grandmother the next day. My parents took me and my brothers and got on a plane that night to travel to Connecticut to visit both of them. I didn't get a chance to tell you where I was going....and the fire happened that night. I was in the hospital for six months after that. My parents sold our house and moved back there to help take care of me—and then I was in rehab for a year. By that time, both my parents had jobs in the area and my two brothers were in school. My parents decided to stay there. I'm so sorry I didn't tell you. I didn't know what to do when I recognized you—and it was so obvious that you didn't recognize me. I thought......I don't know what I thought. I thought I could do this audit and walk away and you would never know. I didn't want you to know...."

I gasp out loud again. "You didn't want me to know?! God—why?! Why would you walk into my life and walk out without even telling me?! Don't you know how much I've missed you?! I haven't gone a day since you left when I haven't missed you and thought about you!"

I break off staring at him. The past and the present collide in another whirlwind of thoughts, ideas, and conflicting timelines.

This is Carter Holt—the studly Health and Safety officer who has been impressing everyone at Howe Firehouse with his poise, professionalism, skill, and thoroughness.

He's also Dylan McNulty—the boy I couldn't live without for my whole childhood. We were inseparable.

I have to struggle to realize that these are the same people.

"I had no idea you felt that way about me," he murmurs. "I had such a massive crush on you during middle school....."

I practically scream and throw myself at him. I fling my arms around his neck, and without thinking, I kiss him. "Dylan! You're back! I missed you so much! I can't wait to tell you everything!"

He doesn't push me away. He kisses me back, but just for a second.

He takes hold of my arms and very gently eases them off his neck. "We can't, Sophie. Believe me—I want to—but we still have a professional relationship—and I'm not ready for that. I'm really flattered that you feel that way, but you don't know what the last fifteen years have been like. I've been ready to spend the rest of my life alone. I'm not ready to start thinking differently—especially if there's a chance it wouldn't work out between us and I'd only be likely to leave here in a few weeks anyway."

I stiffen at those words. I want to argue back that we can never be apart ever again. I've already spent too long away from him.

The next instant, all those thoughts evaporate out of my head. I burst out in relieved laughter. "Okay!" I tell him. "That's all okay. I don't mind. I'm so happy you're here! This is going to be great."

Now it's his turn to blink at me. "You don't mind?"

"Of course not! I don't care! I'm just so happy to get you back—as a friend. We're friends. We'll always be friends. We can keep being friends. We don't have to do anything." I squeal in delight, bounce up and down on the bench, and clap my hands. I even scoot closer to him. "This is going to be so great!" I put my arm around his shoulders and squeeze. "Yay! Dylan!"

"Call me Carter," he tells me in the same undertone. "That's my name now."

I look up at him. "Why? Why did you change your name?"

"There were already four other Dylans in my class when I got out of rehab—and too many people knew about the fire from the news. My parents enrolled me in school under my mother's maiden name. I've been using it ever since."

I stare at the side of his face. He's right. He's Carter now—the strong, self-possessed guy who has been impressing the whole fire crew since he got here.

I can't help but smile at him. "Okay. No problem." I find myself smirking. "This is so great!"

He starts smiling back at me. "I didn't think you would be happy to see me. I thought you would be mad at me for leaving."

"No way! I was never mad at you for leaving. I just really missed you. Losing you.....it was one of the hardest things I ever had to go through." I get another surge of happiness just from looking at him. "I can't believe this!"

He won't stop staring at me. He stares at me the same way he did before—with that deep, searching, unwavering stare. It makes his face look haunted and kind of spooky.

"What?" I ask. "You can't think about walking out of my life again. Don't you dare."

"I wasn't thinking that."

"What are you thinking?"

He hesitates a long time before he replies. When he does, his eyes cast an even more hypnotic spell over me. "I never thought anyone would be this happy to see me. Most people avoid me."

"Stop it!" I tell him. "We're best friends! I would never avoid you! So you got burned. You're still the same person."

"I'm not," he murmurs. "I'm not the same person. I was outgoing then. I had friends. I wasn't this....."

I grab his hand without thinking. "You are the same person! I trust you. Everyone does. You're strong and kind and responsible. I trusted you with my life then and I still do now. You're still the one person I would want in my corner no matter what. You are still the same person. I know you are. You look different—and other people treat you different." I squeeze his hand. "Don't you remember the pact we made before high school? We said we would always stick together no matter what anyone else thought. We said we would be friends and hang out together and go bowling and everything even if no one liked us and everybody else hated us." I can't help but squeeze him. I want to press those words into his hand. "We'll make it like that now. If everyone hates you and avoids you because of the way you look, we'll just treat it like high school and I'll be the one person who doesn't. So there."

He won't stop staring at me. "You really mean that, don't you?"

"Of course! I really needed you back then. You were my foundation. I would have given anything to have you with me each and every day. Nothing has been the same since. You better believe I'm going to do it now—especially since you're the one who needs me. I can't let you go through life thinking you're ugly and unloved. That's ridiculous, Dylan." I cringe. "Sorry."

He won't stop drilling me with those eyes. I don't know how to deal with the way he's looking at me.

"What?" I ask. "What's wrong? If you don't want that...."

"I do," he murmurs. "I want it more than anything."

"Then what's wrong?" I frown up at him. "Something's wrong, isn't it?"

"I'm wrong." He looks away. "I should have said yes when you asked me out."

"You had your reasons and you still do. I can respect that."

Out of nowhere, he squeezes my hand back. I only took his hand as a friend. That squeeze means something else now.

"I want to go out with you, Sophie," he murmurs. "I just.....I don't know how to."

I burst out laughing. "That's easy! We'll go bowling like we used to. We don't have to make it a massive date or anything. We're just friends."

He tries to smile and fails. God, he looks so sad! The last years must have been torture for him. "Okay," he husks. "I'd really like that."

I can't stop laughing from sheer happiness. "So do you want me to pick you up?"

He smirks once before he remembers that he's supposed to be serious. "I know how to drive. I'll pick you up."

I laugh again and lean over to bump my shoulder into him. "I'm so happy to see you! Everything seems so much better, now that you're here."

"I really didn't know how you would react," he murmurs.

I shake my head. "I'm sorry if I made you think that...."

"You didn't. It was just my own fear talking. I told myself things could never go back to the way they were. I told myself you would have moved on—or that you would resent me for not contacting you—or that you would be married and your husband wouldn't want me in your life. I thought a lot of things." He looks away. "I guess it was a typical high school crush situation. I thought there was no way in hell you would ever feel that way about me again after all this time."

"I don't feel that way about you because I didn't have a crush on you then. You were just my friend." I laugh and nudge him again. "I have a massive crush on you now, though."

He glances at me, and this time, I definitely see his skin color. It looks different from a regular blush because of his burns.

"You're really serious, aren't you—about all that stuff about me being attractive?"

"Absolutely!" I exclaim. "Haven't you looked in the mirror lately?"

He grimaces. "I have to do it every day. Maybe we're talking about two different people."

"We obviously are. You're talking about the person on the outside and I'm talking about the person on the inside—but even so, the person on the outside is still unbelievably attractive. Look at you! You're strong. You're healthy. You're a natural leader. You're in charge of everything. Jesus, anyone who can tell John Brewer what to do must be a natural leader."

He gives a nervous little laugh. "He's a pussy cat underneath it all."

"He may be a pussy cat, but he's still the boss."

We go back to staring at each other. His existence makes me indescribably happy.

I can't believe this is happening! Dylan is back! My whole life looks brighter. All the shadows seem to be fading away.

I want to jump up and down and dance and cheer all at the same time. Every dark moment of my life vanishes as if it never happened. He's here. He's sitting right in front of me.

He sees me grinning and tries unsuccessfully to stay serious. "What?" he asks.

I beam at him. "Nothing. I'm just looking at you."

"You're really pretty," he murmurs. "You sure are beautiful."

"So are you," I half-whisper. "I can't believe you grew up into this. You're such a prize."

He gulps and tears spring to his eyes. "I missed you so much, Sophie."

My throat tightens and my eyes sting. "I missed you, too, Dylan. You don't know how happy I am to see you again."

We both attack each other in a crushing hug at the same time. I can't let go of him.

"Don't leave!" I blurt out in his ear. Tears streak down my cheeks. "Don't leave when you finish this audit. I can't lose you again!"

"I don't want to," he husks. "I don't want to leave. I just…..I don't know how it would work."

I push him back and see tears on his cheeks, too. "Just promise me we won't lose each other again. I can't go through that again."

"Okay," he chokes. "I don't want to go through that again, either. Let's just….let's see how it goes for the rest of the audit. Then we'll decide what to do."

I nod fast. "Okay." I dive in and kiss him on the cheek. "I'm just so happy to see you again. I can't face losing you again."

"Let's not talk about that anymore. Let's just go bowling and have some fun the way we used to."

"Okay!" I laugh and wipe my tears away.

Then we both go back to sitting next to each other holding hands and staring into each other's eyes.

I don't know what else to say to him. I don't know how I can ever walk away from him again. I want to take him home and keep him there forever.

"I should probably go," he rasps. "If I don't go now, I'll never be able to."

I laugh again. "Yeah. I feel the same way."

"When is your next day off? You have tomorrow off, don't you?"

"Yeah. Then I'm back on for five days."

"We better go out tomorrow, then. How about I pick you up and seven?"

I burst into a huge grin. "Great. I'll see you then."

He doesn't get up to leave right away. He stares into my eyes for a long time.

He finally squeezes my hand, whispers, "Bye," and walks away into the park.

He leaves me sitting there with my head reeling. Dylan is back. I can't believe it.

Then I remember. We're going out tomorrow night. Yay! This is going to be great!

Chapter 12: Carter

I pull into the firehouse for my shift and pretend not to see that I'm rostered on the same rotation with Andy Skinner again.

I get straight to work. I'm way too happy about going bowling with Sophie tomorrow night. I don't have time to let anything bring me down.

I can't believe she's actually happy to see me after everything that's happened.

She told me that story at the beach about getting depressed and losing all her drive and direction in life after I left.

I thought she would be furious when she found out I'm her long-lost friend whose disappearance caused her all that suffering.

I still find it hard to believe her reaction. She actually likes me. She doesn't just want to be friends. She actually thinks I'm attractive. She called me a prize.

She's one in a million—but I already knew that way back when we were kids. I knew then that I would never meet anyone else like her—and I was right.

I don't think she even sees my scars.

No, she definitely sees them. She just finds them attractive instead of ugly. She can't believe I think I'm ugly or that anyone else would.

I also have a hard time making eye contact with Jessie and some of the other female members of the fire crew. Sophie said Jessie thinks I'm hot. Who else around here thinks that?

I don't want to know. I concentrate on spending my time with the male firefighters I know like me.

Luckily for me, most of them are already married. I don't have to worry about going wrong there.

I go through the truck checks with Vince, Theo, Billy, and Danny. Then we all go up to the breakroom to relax. We'll be sleeping in the bunkroom all night—or at least until we get a call.

Andy avoids me like he might have actually grown a few brain cells in the last twenty-four hours.

What an idiot he is for mistreating Sophie. He had her in the palm of his hand and he drove her away. He doesn't deserve her.

I could throttle the jackass for hurting her—and for lying to me about them still being together.

I don't have to throttle him because she delivered an epic takedown harder than any I could ever give him.

He doesn't shoot off his mouth so much to the rest of the crew. Sophie is right about him. Now everyone knows what a dipshit he is.

No one trusts him. No one likes him. No one even tries to rely on him.

He shouldn't be on the fire crew. That's the truth. I would fire the son of a bitch if I was in Chief Brewer's place. I wouldn't keep Andy around to poison the crew.

I've seen Chief Brewer's crew roster, though. He doesn't really have a choice about keeping Andy on. Chief Brewer is lucky if he manages to fill all his shifts with enough people every week.

He's been advertising non-stop for over two years—ever since Ellen Foreman got hurt.

It took over a year before Josh hired on. Now Leila is out on indefinite maternity leave.

I can see Chief Brewer's point about Andy's attitude. It's a problem, but he still performs professionally—just well enough to keep his job. Chief Brewer can't really afford to fire him—not unless Andy does something really bad.

I hate to let it go as far as that, but I can't really do anything about it. I already did my part by getting Chief Brewer to file a disciplinary reprimand against Andy.

He seems to be taking my warning to heart, so maybe he isn't completely brain dead after all—or maybe he just knows when to behave when he's worried about getting caught.

I try to put him out of my mind and think about going out with Sophie tomorrow. This is not a date. This is not a date. This is not a date. I have to keep telling myself that.

God, I had it bad for her in high school! I dreamed about her every night. Spending time with her all day every day didn't help, either.

I still find it hard to believe she's grown up into such a knockout—and she likes me of all people.

I drift off into a daydream when the fire alarm goes off. I struggle to come back to reality as the whole crew tumbles downstairs.

I climb into the rescue truck. Keith and the usual day crew aren't here on the night shift.

Billy drives. Danny sits in the seat next to him. Vince and Theo sit with me in the back seat.

Jessie and Andy are our paramedics in the rescue truck. We all scramble into our turnouts while Danny pulls up the dispatch notes.

"Robbery gone wrong in a convenience store downtown!" he yells over the siren. "Four patients—Police on scene!"

"What—no vehicles involved?" Theo calls forward. "Are you sure you can't order a few semis to run through the front window while we're at it?"

Danny makes a face at him over his shoulder. "Carter is sitting right here listening, dumbass. I'm sure he'll be watching to make sure the Police angle all their squad cars to block off the scene."

I find myself laughing. "I'm not here to audit the Police."

"And you don't order up what kind of calls we get, either, do you?" Danny winks at Theo. "Nice try, though. Keep wishing."

"While you're at it, how about you start wishing we get back to the station at a decent hour so we can get some sleep?" Billy asks and pulls out onto the road.

The two trucks and two ambulances roll into town. We come to a Police barricade long before we get to the scene. They escort us through all the jammed traffic to the convenience store in question.

The gunmen are long gone, and sure enough, the Police have the whole store surrounded in squad cars. We have to wait for them to pull out of the way so we can get close enough to the store entrance.

Chief Brewer shows up and the whole crew piles out. The regular firefighters make a circuit of the area while the paramedics go inside and find the four patients lying on the floor.

A dozen Police officers stand around inside the destroyed store to secure the scene.

Andy and Jessie take one patient. Chris and Josh are rostered together on the ladder truck. They go to work on one patient together.

Brooke and Naomi are on the two ambulances working with EMTs George Dow and Drew Killian.

I triage the patients. Andy's and Jessie's patient is the most critical. He's the store clerk with three through-and-through gunshot wounds to his chest.

He already has two qualified paramedics working on him, so I go help Naomi with the second-most critical.

The patient is an old lady who happened to walk through the door just as the gunmen were trying to escape after shooting the clerk and two other customers.

The old lady got in the attackers' way at the wrong place and the wrong time. They shot her once in the head.

The bullet hit her in the temple, cracked her skull, and glanced off. The bullet carved a path through the side of her head, but her skull protected her well enough.

The gunshot wound isn't as serious as it could be. She would have made a full recovery from that, but the gunmen also knocked her over when they shoved past her to get away.

They pushed her against one of the nearby magazine racks. She lost her balance—made worse by the gunshot wound, of course—and sustained another head injury when she fell.

Naomi and I have our work cut out for us treating her head injuries and her spiking blood pressure. Drew and the firefighters try to secure her spine and load her onto the gurney.

The worst part of this call is that we don't have enough extra people to help out. If this was the day crew, we could call in the second shift to lend a hand.

Chief Brewer winds up helping out and he recruits a few Police officers who have EMT certification, too.

He gives orders to the firefighters to prioritize Andy's and Jessie's patient first and then mine.

Naomi and I work seamlessly in a perfectly synchronized concert of orders, information, suggestions, and rapidly changing strategies as our patient deteriorates.

We don't have a minute to take our hands off the old lady. We're still working as fast as we can when Drew and the firefighters finally load her onto a gurney and we head for the door.

Andy and Jessie get there before us with their patient on another gurney. Their patient must have coded because Danny rides on the gurney's lowest bar while he does compressions in between defibrillations.

Andy walks along at the patient's head. He has intubated the patient and he carries the oxygen tank in one hand while he pumps the ventilator bag with his other hand.

Normally, we put the oxygen tank on the gurney with the patient—either next to their body or between their legs.

That isn't possible here because the paramedics have also applied a MAST suit to compensate for the patient losing so much blood.

There isn't room on the gurney on top of Danny doing compressions and Jessie injecting drugs into the patient's IV.

Naomi and I hang back to let Andy's crew get through the door first. I don't see how the gurney can get through that narrow doorway with so many people working around the patient.

I'm just about to call up there and suggest that they unlock and open the second door just next to it. That will make enough space for them and us to get outside.

Right at that moment, one of the Police officers on guard slips in a puddle of the patient's blood.

The officer tries to catch his balance, starts to topple, and flails his arms out to grab the nearest thing he can reach to stabilize himself.

He's in a completely different aisle from Andy and his patient, but the officer falls into a nearby shelf and it wobbles.

A bunch of half-gallon soda bottles cascade off the shelf and fall right on top of the oxygen tank in Andy's hand.

Naomi and I are standing right behind Andy's crew. We see the whole disaster unfold. Even Chief Brewer is standing right there and witnesses the whole damn thing.

The soda bottles strip the oxygen tank out of Andy's hand. He tries to take his other hand off the ventilator bag in time to grab the tank, but it's too late.

The tank hits the floor right on top of its regulator valve, snaps off the valve, and the tank explodes. It fires across the floor, hits the gurney with Andy's patient strapped to a backboard on top of it, and the whole shooting match goes down in a blaze of glory.

The gurney crashes down sideways on the floor and the patient falls off still strapped to his backboard. He couldn't fall in a worse possible position for someone with his injuries.

The fall comes perilously close to tearing out the ET tube in his mouth, but it does tear out the oxygen tubing hooked up to the ventilator bag.

Andy dives for the gurney and manages to keep bagging the patient all the way down even though he's only bagging with plain air now.

Danny falls off the gurney, hits the IV tubing, and tears that out, too. Jessie tries to grab the IV, misses, and barely manages to grab his arm in time.

She clamps her thumb over the bloody hole in his vein and holds it to stop him from losing any more blood.

She winds up tripping over Danny and they both go down, but she still doesn't let go.

I open my mouth to start giving orders, but Andy reacts first and starts yelling at everyone around him. "Get another oxygen tank from the ambulance, Theo! Get him back on the gurney and stabilize his C-spine precautions! Tape up his arm, Jessie, and start another IV! We need to profuse him on the double!"

Naomi and I stand back out of the way. Our patient is just as critical, but I don't say a word while the two paramedics and all the extra firemen work their tails off to get the patient back on the gurney and hooked up to a fresh supply of oxygen.

Jessie starts an IV in a different site on the patient's hand and goes back to shooting him full of drugs.

Danny drags himself out of the danger zone, but he must have hurt himself, too. He doesn't stand up.

Chief Brewer goes over there to talk to him and then leaves him there while they finish angling the patient out of the store.

They load him into an ambulance and disappear into the night. Naomi and I have our hands full with our own patient. I don't see Andy and Jessie again until Drew drives me and Naomi to the hospital.

I happen to glance out into the convenience store parking lot before Drew slams the door with us inside.

The last thing I see is Chief Brewer supporting Danny on his shoulder and helping Danny limp across the parking lot to Chief Brewer's pickup.

Naomi and I are too busy working on our patient to talk to Andy or Jessie once we hand off to the medical team at the hospital. Then all four of us have to race back to the scene to transport the other two patients.

They aren't as critical, and by the time we come back from our second trip, Danny is lying on another bed in the Emergency Department.

Chief Brewer comes over to me once I finish the last hand-off. "I think you might have a problem, man," he tells me.

"I'm not taking any more of those this decade. Come back twenty years from now."

He tries to smile and fails. "Andy thinks you're going to try to pin this on him."

I look up. "Pin what on him?"

"The whole oxygen tank disaster. He thinks you're going to make it out that it was his fault for not securing the tank."

I frown at him. "I know it wasn't his fault. There was no way to secure the tank and he had no reason to believe he was in any danger of dropping it."

He only shrugs. "I'm just warning you. Be careful. He's on a hair trigger."

He walks away and leaves me alone with my paperwork and my thoughts. Fantastic. Just fantastic.

A defensive paramedic who thinks I'm out to get him—that's the last thing I need right now.

Chapter 13:
Carter

I have to seriously control my heart rate when I walk up to Sophie's apartment door.

She lives in a very nice apartment complex on the north side of Howe—the nice side.

Her building has a sweeping staircase rising from the lobby, a shiny modern silver elevator with electronic buttons, and the halls between apartments all have nice deep red carpet and wall sconces on the walls.

I ring the doorbell on her apartment and then squirm in my clothes while I wait for her to answer.

I had to be careful about looking good for this, but not too good. This is not a date. This is not a date. This is not a date.

Sophie and I are just friends. She's my subordinate at the firehouse. We're just hanging out casually the same way we did at the barbecue. This is just a night of friendly enjoyment—nothing else.

I decide to wear a pair of jeans and a navy T-shirt with a brown wool blazer over it. I don't look like I'm all dressed up to go on a date, but I don't look like I'm slumming it going bowling with my best friend, either.

Hopefully she won't read too much into my clothes. What is she going to show up in? I hope she doesn't come too dressed up. That would make this feel too much like a date.

I also hope she does dress up. I want to see how stunning she looks when she isn't wearing her uniform or the casual blouses and slacks she wore to the beach and to the park.

She yanks open the apartment door from the inside and bursts into a giant grin when she sees me. Her eyes brighten when they dip to my clothes.

The apartment behind her is large, modern, and fancy. She keeps it immaculately clean with nothing out of place.

Big windows cover the living room wall behind her. They look out over a courtyard in the middle of the apartment complex. Trees surround a pool and cabana out there. This place is really nice.

I only see that for a split second before I see her in all her magnificence. A black clip holds part of her blonde hair behind her neck.

Stray wisps drape around her face and from her ears to spill over her shoulders.

She wears a casual little beige dress with tiny maroon flowers sprinkled all over it. The short puffy sleeves barely cover her shoulders, run vertically down to her armpits in a square bodice, and then cut straight across her chest to the other side.

The dress doesn't show any cleavage, but it can't do anything to hide the full curvaceous beauty of her bust underneath. The dress actually seems to enhance it.

String bow ties scrunch the rest of the dress tight around her sides, breasts, hips, and bare thighs.

It's the most innocent, casual, friend-date dress I can possibly imagine, but it also makes her look impossibly hot. I have to force myself to stop staring at her chest, hips, ass, and waist.

She wears an innocuous pair of half-height strappy sandal heels that make her look even more like a runway model. Am I really going out with this goddess?

Her dress slithers around her body with every move she makes. It's the sultriest, most seductive look and it drives me wild—but I'm not thinking about that. I'm not going on a date with her. We're just friends, remember?

Her cheeks flush. That color washes down her neck to her chest and up to her ears. I can just imagine how other parts of her body turn red like that when she gets excited.

"You look really nice," she half-whispers.

"You look outstanding." I do my best to keep my voice calm. "You look stunning."

She blushes again. "Are you ready to go?"

"Yeah." I turn the other way and head back toward the elevator.

She pulls the apartment door closed to lock it and slips a code card into her little black clutch.

She won't stop beaming at me all the way down the hall, in the elevator, outside to my truck while I open the door for her to get in, and on our way into town.

I feel her staring at me from the passenger seat. "Is something wrong?" I ask. "Do I have mousse in my hair?"

She bursts out laughing. "I would tell you if you did." She stretches out her hand and squeezes my arm through my jacket while I drive. "I'm just really happy that you're here. I can't believe I'm actually going out with you and we're all grown up and everything."

I feel my throat starting to constrict. I can't look at her or I really will lose it. I pay attention to the road instead.

"I can't believe it, either," I tell her. "I feel like I'm in another dimension or something—one I only dreamed about before."

She sighs, faces front, and settles back in her seat. I can't even look toward her side of the truck or I'll start fantasizing about her.

"This whole thing is like a fairy tale," she murmurs. "I keep waiting to wake up and find out it isn't real."

I take a chance, cover her hand with mine, and squeeze it tighter into my arm. I need to feel her. "It's real. All of this is really happening."

"Tell me more about what happened to you. I want to know everything you've been doing since I saw you last."

"There isn't a lot to tell. I was lying flat on my back in a hospital bed in a morphine haze for six months after that nightmare Thanksgiving." I glance over at her. "I hate Thanksgiving now. Just warning you."

She laughs and her eyes twinkle at me across the seat. "I'll make a note of that. I really don't blame you. Go on. Then what?"

"Then rehab—which wasn't a lot different. It took me a long time to be able to walk and move around and just function. It took almost a full year before my skin got thick enough that I could move at all without tearing it and reinjuring myself."

She flinches. "That sounds awful."

"It was. It was excruciating. My parents only visited me on the weekends because it was too hard for them to watch me suffering so much. My mom used to get really emotional. She always broke down crying every time she visited me. She once told me in tears that she was really sorry but visiting me was just too hard because she wanted so badly to help me and she couldn't. After a while, my brothers stopped visiting completely. My mom said they just needed to get back to living normal lives—and I understood that. I never held it against them."

"Wow," she breathes. "I wish I could have done something for you then. I wish I had known. I would have....well, I don't know what I would have done. I would have written you letters or something—anything to make you know that I still thought of you and cared about you."

I can't look at her. "I couldn't have called you or written to you until I got out of the hospital. By then, so much time had passed that I thought you wouldn't want to hear from me again." I look the other way to stare out of the driver's window. "I thought you would be so mad at me for disappearing out of your life."

She crushes my arm under her hand. "I'm just glad you're okay. I'm so glad you survived the fire. I'm glad for all of it so I could see you again."

I can't speak. She means more to me than anything.

I keep my hand on top of hers. I have to feel her touching me. I won't believe any of this is real if I don't keep feeling her right here next to me.

"Then what happened?" she asks. "What happened after you got out of rehab?"

"I went home. I got out of rehab in May of what would have been my sophomore year in high school. I stayed at home over summer vacation and just spent that time recovering and learning to move around and function some more. Then I started high school in my junior year."

She doesn't ask how bad it was. I don't think I could talk about that.

"My brothers had a really hard time when I started school. People harassed them about me—called me names to my brothers' faces and they got into fights because of me. It was all typical high school stuff—but my being there made life harder for them. My younger brother had a really hard time. He eventually had an outburst at home and said point blank that he wished I hadn't survived the fire because I ruined their whole family. My parents got really upset, but they wound up moving my brothers to other schools where no one knew about me. Everyone at that school already knew about me, so my parents left me there."

"I'm so sorry you had to go through that," she breathes.

"I didn't *have* to go through it. My parents offered to let me home-school for the last two years of high school and do all the courses remotely. I turned them down."

"Why?!" she gasps. "Why would you willingly put yourself through that?"

"I thought I needed it. I spent all this time learning how to function. I learned how to cook. I learned how to handle the over-stimulation of wearing clothes. I learned how to walk and swim and ride a bike. I even learned how to drive. This was the next step—learning how to cope with other people. I knew high school would be bad. I figured, if I could handle that, I could handle anything else."

"You're a lot braver than I would have been," she remarks. "Any lesser person would have hidden away from the world."

"I kinda wanted to stick it in their faces, you know? I wanted to make them look at me whether they wanted to or not. I have to live with this every day. I figured they could suck it up and get used to it. Anyway, it very quickly became a litmus test for who the good people were and which people I could safely eliminate from my life without a backward glance."

"I'll bet you could!" she exclaims. "That must be really convenient for separating the wheat from the chaff."

I find myself smiling at her. "It definitely is."

"Did you patch things up with your brothers in the end?"

"Oh, yeah! They both came back a couple of years later and apologized to me for all the things they said. They were both extremely ashamed of the way they acted, especially my younger brother, but I didn't mind. I understood exactly how they felt and he was right. The fire did ruin their family. It really would have been better for all four of them if I died in the fire. They all could have moved back to that house and gone on with their lives instead of getting dragged through decades of hell. My recovery completely ruined my parents."

"Ruined them how?"

"It just wrecked them emotionally. They were both so vital and energetic before. You remember how they were. The whole process just crushed them both. They both became sad, depressed, hollow shells of their former selves. They still haven't recovered completely even though they can see that I'm fine. That's one of the reasons I decided to move away to the other side of the country. They needed a break from seeing me and being constantly reminded of everything that happened to me."

She shakes her head. "That is an incredible story. You really have come a long way."

I pull into the bowling alley parking lot just then. I can finally turn to her, but I have to stop myself from grabbing her, kissing her, and mauling her right here in the truck.

"Okay, that's enough of that," I tell her. "No more gloomy stories from the past. We're here to enjoy ourselves, not to mope around."

She bursts into a bright grin and gives me a fake military salute. "Yes, Sir. Order received and acknowledged. My lips are sealed."

I glance down at her mouth at those words. I really hope her lips aren't sealed, but we aren't thinking about that.

She won't stop grinning when I get out, walk around the truck, and open the door for her. She smirks at me all the way inside—and halfway across the parking lot, she slips her hand into my elbow to take my arm.

She only blushes and smiles at me when I look over at her. Holy Christ, she feels good on my arm like this! Are we on a date after all?

Chapter 14:
Sophie

I can't believe how happy I am walking into the bowling alley with Carter. It might have been better for his family if he died in the fire, but then I wouldn't be experiencing this moment right now.

I keep finding myself glancing over at him and smirking. He does the same thing, but his lips don't quite respond the way they should.

I don't care because I understand his facial expressions now. His eyes show how happy he is even if his mouth doesn't function the way a normal mouth would.

I'm starting to see how really different he is from the friend I used to have. He's right that Dylan is gone, but in the best possible way.

Carter is so much more self-possessed. He has a bigger personality. He's more confident than Dylan was.

Carter has to put himself out there every day to be stared at, pointed at, mocked, and for little children to run screaming from him in fear.

I can only imagine the nightmare he went through in high school—and he did it deliberately to prove himself. I can't imagine Dylan doing anything like that.

It's no wonder Carter is so self-assured. He's been through so much and come out on top.

We get even more stares when we walk into the bowling alley—even more than he would probably get if he went by himself.

People whisper to each other about us. They're probably asking themselves how a monster like him can be going out with a beautiful woman who obviously fawns all over him.

I realize standing next to him how good I look. I always get a lot of attention from men when I clean myself up and go out.

I know I'm society's definition of good-looking, but the contrast between me and Carter makes it so much more obvious that he isn't.

My heart swells with pride when I see people looking at the two of us together. We aren't technically together, but it sure feels good to make people see him as that.

Maybe now they'll realize how exceptional he is. He deserves to walk into a public place with a beautiful woman on his arm. He deserves to have people realize he must be something outstanding to get a woman like that.

I sure wish it could be me, but I can live with it if it isn't. It will be enough for me if I just make him understand the possibility.

I can't stand the idea of him going through life alone because of some unfortunate accident. He's been through enough. He deserves to be happy even if he can't get it from me.

We sign in at the counter and rent our bowling shoes. He laughs at me when I change out of my heels. "You would look nicer if you bowled in those."

I smirk at him. "You're only saying that so you can see me fall over the first time I bowl a lane."

He scowls at the rack full of balls. "You won't fall over, but I probably will. I haven't bowled since the last time you and I went together."

I gape at him. "You haven't?! Why not?! We always bowled when we were younger."

"That was always something you and I did together. I never bowled with anyone else. After the accident, I had enough to deal with just learning how to hold a fork and getting to the bathroom by myself. Bowling was pretty far down on the priority list—and after that, I never had anyone to go with. It fell through the cracks, I guess." He cocks his head to look at me. "Have you bowled a lot?"

I nod. "I went all the time after you left. I used to go by myself and pretend you were there. It was one of the ways I used to remember you when I felt lonely and like no one else wanted me around."

He turns back to rolling the balls around on the rack. "I am so sorry that happened to you. I would have given anything to go through high school with you the way we planned."

"We aren't talking about that, remember?" I push him out of the way and pick up my ball. "Choose your weapon. It's time to bowl."

He selects his ball, pulls off his jacket, and lays it on the bench next to our chosen lane.

We log into the computer scoring system, but I only enter one name. *Sophiedylan*.

We always used that name when we bowled back then. We never bowled to win. We just bowled our lanes and added up both scores into one so we could both call it a win.

Carter grins when he sees the name, but he doesn't comment on it. "You can go first," he tells me. "You can show me how it's done."

I take my bowl to the top of the lane, wind up, and send my ball down the lane. I get a strike the very first time.

He whistles through his teeth. "Pretty impressive."

I grin at him while I wait for my ball to come back. "I'm sure you'll do just fine. You were a really good bowler back then. Don't think I don't remember."

He won't stop smiling. His scars turn that darker shade of red that tells me he's blushing.

I bowl my second frame and get a seven. He stands up and I sit down.

He looks even more impressive in his T-shirt when he picks up his ball, adjusts his grip, and takes his stance at the top of the lane.

He executes a perfect bowl and gets another strike. I cheer from the sidelines. "Woo-hoo! I knew you could do it! You haven't lost your touch."

He blushes again and concentrates on getting his ball back. My yelling attracts attention from all over the bowling alley. People stop what they're doing to watch Carter bowl his second frame.

He gets another strike. "You're lucky we aren't keeping score," he tells me when he sits down next to me.

"Don't tell me you've gotten all competitive since you were younger."

"I wouldn't know because I always do solo sports. This is the first time I've done anything with someone else—but I could see it getting really competitive."

"Well, we aren't doing that. We're here to enjoy ourselves."

He beams at me. "I am enjoying myself—a lot."

Now it's my turn to blush. I stand up and feel his eyes on me when I pick up my ball. I bowl a seven and use my second ball to clean up the rest. I'm the one who says this isn't competitive, but I feel myself starting to fall behind.

We finish bowling our game and congratulate each other on our win.

"What do you want to do now?" I ask.

"Let's go get ice cream like we used to."

I glance down at his muscular chest and arms. "Are you sure you're allowed that? Are you on a strict bodybuilding diet or anything?"

He laughs. "Call me inspired because I'm out with you. I want to relive the fondest memories of my childhood."

I gaze at him in wonder and genuine affection. "We sure had some good times back then, didn't we?"

He gazes back and his eyes go hard and intense again when he looks at me. "Yeah. We sure did. You were the best thing about my childhood. I'll always be grateful to you for that. The best times of my childhood were always with you."

I want to put my arms around him, but I stop myself. Fortunately, we get to the ice cream stand just then.

We both get our ice cream in cups the way we used to. We take our ice cream outside and sit on a bench overlooking the minigolf course.

People putt around the course. They don't pay any attention to us.

Carter and I eat our ice cream in silence for a while. I'm not sure what to say to break that silence.

I want to bombard him with questions about his past. I want to catch up on every day and every detail of the time I missed.

I also want to unload on him so he knows every detail of every day when he wasn't with me.

It somehow seems important that I download all this information into him. I want to put everything back to the way it was as if he never left.

He doesn't want that, though. I don't want to spoil the nice time we're having by talking about the past.

I can't talk about the future, either. I don't know if we'll have one. I don't even want to talk about the present. I don't want to spend tonight talking about work.

I glance over at him at the same time he glances over at me. I'm just putting a spoonful of ice cream in my mouth and I smirk at him when I do.

His eyes drop to my mouth—and he doesn't smile back. His expression goes hard.

He leans over, scoops some of my ice cream out of my cup with his spoon, and raises it to put it in my mouth.

His eyes never leave my mouth when I close my lips on the spoon and suck the ice cream off it.

He glances up into my eyes and then back down to my mouth.

My world stops when he leans forward a second time, slips his hand behind my back, and pulls me toward him to kiss me on the bench.

His lips feel cold and taste sweet. They also feel thin and hard—not soft and plushy like normal human lips.

He kisses me deep and strong. His lips somehow feel more demanding and insistent—not pliant or romantic or subtle.

The power of that kiss stops my heart and my breath. He doesn't do anything by half-measures and he doesn't kiss by half-measures, either. He goes all the way in and demands my lips for himself.

His hands and arms wrap around my waist from behind and pull me in tighter than I would expect from a first kiss.

He doesn't do any of this tentatively or questioningly or uncertainly. He knows exactly what he wants and he takes it.

I gasp in his mouth as he pulls me closer. I have to scoot along the bench to move into his arms.

He doesn't release his hold on my lips when he swings one leg over the bench so he sits straddling it.

He pulls me between his knees, runs his hand up the back of my dress to my neck, and his fingers clench in my hair.

His hold makes me melt in his hands. My heart turns a somersault as excitement takes over.

The fingers of his other hand crawl around my waist and squeeze just above my hip in such an explicit suggestion. I shiver with excitement and arch my back into his embrace.

Almost as if he's waiting for me to react like that, he eases off. He delivers a few smaller, softer kisses to my lips, straightens up, and his arms trail off me as he lets me go.

"Mmmm," he murmurs. "Your lips taste like ice cream."

I can't stop panting in breathless trembling anticipation. I want him so bad. Everything about him turns me on.

"What was that for?" I gasp. "You said you weren't ready for it."

"I'm not. I just really wanted to kiss you." He strokes his fingertips down my neck, drags them across the bare skin of my chest above the top of my dress, and studies the interplay of color and reactions crossing my face. "I wanted to see you like this."

I can barely breathe. "Like what?" I gasp.

"I wanted to see how much you want me." He glides his hand back up and rests it very lightly around my neck from the front. "I wanted to see that you're really mine if I want to take you."

I explode out in a panting, gasping moan at the way he's touching me. He's barely touching me at all, but his eyes hold me enthralled.

Is he just playing with me to make me react? Will he let me down as soon as he proves to himself that I wasn't lying about finding him attractive?

He takes his hand away like it never crossed his mind to do anything like that.

Chapter 15: Sophie

I want to cry when Carter turns away from me, picks up his ice cream cup, and makes a slow, deliberate show of scooping out a spoonful of ice cream.

No way can he kiss me like that and just leave me broken and aching for him. My whole body quivers with tension. I want to throw myself at him, but it won't do any good.

Very slowly, he looks up at me and raises the spoonful of ice cream to my lips. I open my mouth and he watches my lips close around the spoon when I suck the ice cream off.

I can't move. I can only sit here entranced while his eyes trace my lips. He glances up into my eyes once.

I know exactly what he's doing now and it drives me insane. He is so unbelievably magnetic. Everything about him is strong and hard and impossibly hot. He holds me in the palm of his hand and he knows exactly what he's doing.

He takes the spoon out of my mouth and very slowly, ever-so-se-ductively, he drags the smooth back curved side of the ice-cold spoon down my neck to my chest.

He teases my skin to screaming madness when he passes the spoon back and forth across my chest and then down to my breasts.

He rubs the spoon very lightly over my breasts through my dress—just enough to tease my nipples to rock-hard sensitivity.

He never looks away from my eyes. He reads every quiver of my lips when I gasp and moan and spasm at the intensity of the sensation. He seems to enjoy making me react like this.

"I used to dream about you so much back then, baby," he half-whispers. His voice drifts into my fogged brain from somewhere else. "You were the one I fantasized about every day all the way through high school. I dreamed of doing so many things to you....and experiencing your body in every possible way....."

I sob in misery when he takes the spoon away, but he doesn't stop touching me.

His hands squeeze my sides again, stroke up my arms to my shoulders, cup the back of my neck, and then run down to my hips and finally to my thigh.

His strong, possessive fingers squeeze my thigh through my dress and make me whimper.

I don't want him to stop. I want him to pull me into his lap right here in front of all the golfers on the minigolf course.

He won't do that, though. I know he won't do anything inappropriate. He might not do anything at all. He might just kiss me and touch me like this and then drop it. That would be the truly professional thing to do—and he's always the professional.

I can't stop clawing at his arms and shoulders while he touches me. I'm too overwrought to do anything else.

When he decides he's done touching me, he pulls me in and kisses me again. His touch leaves me trembling with so much buried desire.

I want him more than anything, but I'll still be okay if he decides not t o.

I find myself touching his head, neck, and cheeks while we kiss. His skin fascinates me. It feels so different from normal human skin, but it somehow makes him so much more appealing like this.

No one else has ever touched him like this. I want to admire all his scars. They make him who he is. They make him strong and self-possessed and so unique. No one else in the world has his combination of experiences.

He eases back to gaze into my eyes and runs his fingers through my hair. He keeps looking around at my hair, my lips, my neck, my face, and everything else.

I see him appreciating what he sees. He thinks I'm beautiful.

I just want to hug him—and everything else.

I put my arms around his neck to hug him, but our positions on this bench make it uncomfortable for both of us.

He wraps his arms around me and then, in answer to my prayers, he scoops one arm under my knees and lifts me onto his lap.

He holds me there while we kiss. His arms and hands rocket me into a whole new dimension of desire and excitement. He's hard inside his pants, but he doesn't try to dig it into me. I can't even tell if he wants me to know it's there.

I want to turn around, straddle him, and ride him right this minute, but I don't want to take it further than he's ready to go.

He keeps gripping my waist, my hips, and my thighs. He scoops his powerful hands up to my ribs and then cradles my face while we kiss.

He slips his fingers into my hair and clenches his fist.

All those movements add up to such a seductive tide of throbbing heat between my legs. I want him to slip his hand between my thighs and finger me. I want him to sit me on his lap naked and take me like this.

I want to rock in his arms reeling in ecstasy, but I still don't know if he even wants to go there.

Maybe he just wants to check that he can. Maybe he just wants to prove to himself that some woman wants him enough to respond to him like this.

Just then, one of the workers goes out onto the minigolf course and holds a loud conversation with some of the customers playing there.

It isn't a hostile or confrontational conversation. It's just louder than the bubble of voices coming from the course before now.

The sound snaps both Carter and me out of our trance. He puts me back down on the bench and we both go back to finishing our ice cream.

Neither of us says anything else until we finish. We stand up and throw our empty cups in the trash. We add our dirty spoons to the tub under the counter.

Carter waits for me while I go to the bathroom. When I come out, he slips his hand into mine and squeezes.

I could still consider that a friendly squeeze, but he doesn't let go.

I see what we must look like from the outside. Everyone sees us holding hands and making out like we're a couple.

I sure wish we were. I don't ever want Dylan to leave ever again. I can't imagine ever getting together with another guy after this. He's the only one I've ever wanted.

I understand that now. I felt that way about him back then in high school. I just didn't know enough to realize I felt that way about him.

My feelings hadn't translated into sexual desire the way his did. I just knew I wanted him by my side every day. I never wanted to lose him.

Those feelings can only lead one direction, now that we're both all grown up.

We head out to his truck. He opens the door for me to get into the passenger seat, but when I sit down and put on my seatbelt, he doesn't shut the door.

He moves in and kisses me a thousand times harder. I'm strapped into the seat, so I can't even put my arms around his neck.

He grabs me much more ravenously and his big, strong hand closes on my breast. He massages it through my dress and makes me whimper into his mouth.

I squirm on the seat in rising need. Doesn't he realize by now how much I need him?

He tries to pinch my nipple through my dress, fails, and before I can stop him, he rips down the low-cut front of my dress, pulls my bra cup down along with it, and dives in to catch my nipple in his mouth.

He sucks hard and I have to stifle a scream. He crushes my ribs right under my breast, pushes me up the seat to take a big mouthful of my breast, and then he blows my mind by grabbing my thigh in one powerful hand.

Before I know what's happening, he pushes my dress up, dives his hand between my legs, and rubs me through my panties.

I really do scream as all this devastating sensation blasts me apart. I writhe and thrash on the seat, but I can't get away.

My hand flies to his bicep, but I can't even reach him in this position. I lie plastered to the seat—completely subjected to all the torrential pleasure and craven lust he's inflicting on me.

He rubs my saturated panties in cruel little circles. I buck my hips into his hand just enough for him to hit my clitoris and I explode in screaming, sobbing orgasm right there on the seat.

I try to struggle against the commanding insistence of his greedy mouth, but he doesn't let me go until I wilt in pathetic trembling ragged hopeless sobs on the seat.

He waits until the very last shuddering moan before he pulls off my breast. He tugs my dress and bra back into place and starts kissing me on the mouth again.

I take a few minutes before I can pull myself together enough to catch up with him. My lips don't respond.

He slips his hand along my ear into my hair to steer my mouth to his—almost as if he's commanding me to kiss him and respond to him the way he wants me to.

I can't stop whimpering and shaking in his hands. Andy never made me orgasm like that. He didn't try very hard.

"I can't keep my hands off you," Carter whispers into my mouth. "I really want to take you home with me right now." His eyes float open. "Will you do that? Will you come home with me?"

I can only moan in response. If he doesn't know by now that I want him, I won't be able to say anything to convince him.

I want to burst into tears and beg him on my knees to take me home and keep me with him always. I don't know how I can even say goodnight to him after this.

"You're so beautiful," he whispers. "You're everything I dreamed you would be. You're an angel."

He kisses me one more time and then kisses me on the forehead before he pulls away.

He still doesn't leave right away. He tugs my dress down my thighs, straightens my top, and goes through a million little actions to make sure I'm settled on the seat where I'm supposed to be.

I look up to find him studying me. Just the sight of the way he's looking at me gives me another spasm of aching desire. Doesn't he know by now how much I want him—how much I love him?

I never let myself use that word when we were growing up together. Dylan was just always there. He was the one constant in my life besides my parents and my brother.

I know now that did love Dylan then. I must have if losing him ruined my life so badly.

I love him now, too. I know that in the bottom corner of my heart.

I love him as a friend, but I love him as more than that. I want him to be the one constant in my life now the way he was back then.

I don't see how that would be possible if we didn't become a couple and spend the rest of our lives together. It's the only solution that makes sense.

I don't tell him that. I don't want to pressure him into something he doesn't feel ready for.

Does he see it? Can he read it in my eyes when I look up at him overflowing with longing for him—for all of him?

He caresses my cheek one more time, shuts the passenger door, and gets behind the wheel. He doesn't look at me or say anything when he starts the motor, steers out of the parking lot, and drives off into town.

Chapter 16:
Carter

A strange, surreal kind of certainty settles over me when I park my truck in the parking lot outside my apartment building.

I look up at the building the same way I have every other time I've come here, but this is different.

Sophie sits next to me in the passenger seat. I did what I said I was going to do. I drove her to my apartment building.

Am I really going to take her upstairs to my apartment and......? I don't have to wonder what will happen once we get there.

She's made it pretty obvious how she feels by the way she responds to me touching her, kissing her, and playing with her body.

She would let me. I don't have to question that. She would do more than let me.

She holds herself back because she doesn't want to make me uncomfortable.

Her whole body vibrates with buried desire. She struggles to contain it. She wants more—a lot more. Am I really ready to give her everything?

I want to, but someone has to be the voice of reason here.

I know what will happen when I take her upstairs to my apartment and I already know I'm going to do it. I just need to sit here and think about it for a minute first.

I look over at her and she stares up at me with that bottomless expression of deep need and longing.

The sight of her eyes glazing over with so much emotion—I can't keep away from her when she looks at me like that.

I lean across the seat and kiss her again. She kisses me back, but she doesn't move on the seat. She shoves herself back into it as tension and breaking agony of desire tears her apart.

She wants me to touch her the way I did in the bowling alley parking lot. She would want me to take her right here in the truck.

I can't do that to her. I can't treat her like a cheap hookup.

I tear myself away before I lose control completely. I have to be careful with her. I have to do this right. I can't let myself do anything to hurt her.

I don't know if there could ever be a chance for us. It doesn't really matter in the end—not tonight.

I want her to remember me and know I did everything to make her feel good. I don't want her to regret anything we do tonight. I want her to look back on tonight as one of the good times.

She doesn't come after me when I stop kissing her. She just sits there staring at me in shocked, abject hunger. Jesus, she is so smoking hot!

I can't look at her when she stares at me like that. I get out of the truck, walk around to her door, and let her out.

She gets out of the truck and stands there waiting while I shut the door. I turn around to lead her inside—and stop in my tracks when I see her shifting her weight in awkward uncertainty.

She doesn't know if she should hold my hand or slip her arm through mine or just stand off to one side—like a stranger or a call girl or some random meaningless hookup I picked up in a bar downtown.

I can't let her think that about me—about us. I don't want her to think I'm using her.

I don't want to turn our friendship into this, but it already seems like it is this. She wants it to be. I want it to be.

Maybe I shouldn't take her upstairs after all. I don't want to get together with her if it will spoil what we already have.

What do we have? We could have something real. I can't imagine ever feeling for anyone else what I feel for her. I don't want to spoil that and I know she feels the same way.

I pull her in and hug her. I just want to make it okay for her. I don't want to do anything to mess this up for her.

My heart bursts when I bury my face in her hair. Her presence floods me with....Is this love? I love her as a friend.

I love her as more than that. I just want her. I want her in my life. I don't want to be alone anymore—and she's the one who always stands by me.

She's been standing by me all these years. I know that now. She never forgot me. She always supported me and cared about me and wished me well.

God damn, my life would have been so different if I only had her to help me get through it. Even just receiving a letter from her once a month would have made a world of difference.

Now she's right here in my arms. She slips her arms around my waist to hug me back.

She quivers all over with tension and desire, but I feel the depth of emotion in her heart at the same time. She doesn't want to lose me as a friend, either. She wants me in her life for the rest of her life even if it's only as a friend.

I kiss the side of her head and pull away determined to give her the choice. I can't push her too hard.

I really want to kiss her on the lips again, but we both know where that leads.

I divert at the last second and kiss her on the forehead instead. "Are you okay with this?" I whisper into her face at close range. "We don't have to do this if you don't want to."

"I do!" Her voice comes out in a cracked, broken whisper with a tiny little scream choked off in the middle. "I want you! You can't do all that to me and leave me like this! I...."

She breaks off and her eyes float up to lock on me with unimaginable power.

"I love you, Dylan!" she chokes in the same agonized rasp. "I want.....I want....."

She falters over the words. Watching her struggle to express herself hurts a lot.

I already know what she wants. I just don't know if I can give it to her.

I pull her in and wind up kissing her again. This kiss turns out to be gentler and more romantic than the others. It doesn't escalate out of control....until it does.

Once I start kissing her, the heat between us explodes the way it did before. I turn her toward the truck and wind up shoving her against it as I devour her mouth. I can't get enough of her.

All the angst and desire I've been keeping bottled up all these years—it won't go back in the bottle, now that I'm finally letting it out.

I never even thought about letting it out before. Now I'm with the one woman I most wanted to give it to.

She doesn't attack me back. I'm going at her too hard. She just accepts it and matches my energy.

She wraps her arms around my neck and kisses me to the ends of the Earth. Holy Christ, her tongue sends forks of lightning through my brain that shoot straight down to my crotch.

She mews into my mouth when I grind her against the truck. Her delicious body undulates against me and she corkscrews her hips into my package like she wants me to take her right now.

I drag my fingertips up her thighs, tug up her skirt, and pull her legs off the ground.

She straps them around me and rides down on me in cruel little hip thrusts. Jesus, she's driving me wild, but I can't do it with her like this. I can't treat her like that.

I ease her feet down so she can stand on her own, but she won't let go of me. She hangs onto me moaning into my mouth and gyrating her hips against me. She's on fire!

I force myself to pull away. I can't look at her when I take her hand or I'll explode right now.

I lead her into the building and unlock the door, but things fall apart again when we get into the elevator.

She turns to face the front the way she's supposed to. I slot in behind her, wrap my arms around her, and bury my face in her neck.

I crawl my mouth up to her ear and pant hard when I feel her ass push against my bulge. She immediately starts squirming under my hands when I touch her and moaning in deep agony.

I scoop up to her breasts and massage them through her dress. I would love to rip it down and feel those succulent orbs drop into my waiting hands.

She pushes them into my grasp and shivers when I bite her neck. She arches into me and her head falls backward onto my shoulder.

Her body feels incredible in my hands. My package throbs so damn hard that it hurts. She makes me ache every time she shoves her ass back into me. She really does want it.

The elevator opens. I'm the one who has to pull away.

She wobbles on unsteady legs when I lead her out of the elevator. I hold her hand, open my apartment door, lead her inside, and shut it behind her.

She starts cruising around the living room looking at everything. My apartment isn't that much different from hers except that the living room windows look out over a busy part of Howe instead of a pool.

She looks at the pictures of my family on the shelf and stops in front of a picture of my parents. "You're right," she murmurs. "They look so much older and more careworn."

I don't want to talk about that. I want to tear her apart right now, but I can't do that.

She knows everything about me. She knows more about me than anyone else in my life.

My parents and brothers are the only other people who know the full story.

They don't know the part of the story with her in it. They only think she was a friend I had a long time ago. They don't know how much she meant to me and how broken up I was to lose her.

I come up behind her again and slip my arms around her waist. I pull her against me, but I don't escalate the way I did before.

I just hold her, nuzzle my face into her neck, and feel her rock in my arms. I want to cry right now, she feels so good.

Her hand flies to my head. Her touch causes such a confused storm of emotions in me. I don't know how to handle the way she touches me

.

No one has ever touched me since the accident—and I don't mean intimately or sexually the way she's touching me now.

Literally no one has touched me—ever. The nurses in the burn unit had to debride my burns every day in the early stages.

No one has touched me since. Ever. My parents hugged me when I got out of rehab, but they made absolutely certain never to touch my skin.

No one has ever touched my face. No one has ever touched my head or my arms.

Her touch sets off so many alarm bells. It brings up so much buried anguish and bad memories—but I don't want to shy away from her in any way.

I want her to touch me—because I know she wants to. She wants to feel my skin because it's mine. She wants to feel how different it is because this is who I am.

I love her for that.

She strokes my scalp and her hand slips down to my neck. I clamp my eyes shut against this torturous whirlwind of emotions.

I bury my face in her neck to hide from how I feel about her, but in a second, she twists out of my arms, turns around, and kisses me.

I wrap my arms around her waist from the front this time. I could push her against the wall and conquer her right here, but holding her and kissing her like this feels so much better.

She keeps stroking my head, the back of my neck, my ears, and my face while we kiss. She keeps her eyes open and looks at every part of my face and head that she can see while she does it.

I know what she's doing. Her eyes widen with wonder and admiration. She actually likes my skin like this. I never thought I would meet anyone like this.

My feelings start to get the better of me. I want to stop kissing her, close my eyes, and just stand here sobbing in agony while she touches me.

I don't want to do that, though. I don't want to make her question if she should be doing this.

Chapter 17: Carter

I pull away, lead Sophie by the hand to the couch, and steer her to sit down next to me. "Do you want anything to eat or drink? I should have taken you out to dinner or at least gotten pizza at the bowling alley. I'm sorry about that. I'm a terrible date."

She laughs and her eyes sparkle when she looks at me. "This wasn't supposed to be a date, remember? It would have been one if you had taken me out to dinner."

She kicks off her heels, folds her feet and legs under her on the side, and leans against the couch cushions next to me as if we're an old married couple talking about our workday.

Sitting in that position makes her waist, hips, and chest curve in the most enticing way. She has no idea how unbelievably hot she is.

She rests her arm on the back of the couch and goes back to stroking my scalp, the back of my neck, my ears, cheeks, and forehead.

I stare into her eyes while she does it and she stares back at me.

She traces every part of me with her hands and her eyes.

I have to kiss this woman. I just want to sit here and bask in the way she's looking at me. She really does find me attractive. I don't want to believe it, but I have to when I see the glow of happiness and wide-eyed amazement in her eyes.

I can't do anything. I know why I brought her here, but I can't bring myself to break that gaze, now that we're both here.

Is this love that I'm feeling for her right now? Is this love that I'm feeling coming from her? It sure feels like it.

I want to say so many things to her, but they all get lost in this mind-blowing feeling. It feels like pain except that it feels too good.

Out of the clear blue sky, she asks, "Did you decide to become a firefighter right after the accident?"

"No, not right away." I have to take a minute to switch my brain back into gear. "I didn't really decide until high school."

"What happened?" she asks. "What made you decide?"

I shrug. I have to think hard to remember anything outside this moment. "I had a meeting with my high school guidance counselor. It was the only meeting I ever had with him and I only went because it was mandatory that we have a career counseling session with the counselor. I didn't want to go and I had no idea what I was going to s ay."

"You wanted to be an architect when you were younger," she reminds me. "You were always drawing pictures of buildings and doing diagrams and stuff back then."

"I lost interest in it when I went to rehab."

"Why?" she asks.

"I don't know. Art wasn't really on my radar while I was in rehab. I had to learn how to write again—which wasn't as hard as the physical therapists made it out to be because my fingers weren't damaged."

She frowns at me, but she never stops caressing my skin. "I don't understand. You could have started up with your art again. It probably would have been easier than becoming a firefighter. Being a firefighter is so physical."

"I guess that's kind of the point, isn't it?"

She furrows her brow at me. "I don't understand."

"I guess it had something to do with changing my name and everything. I became a completely different person. I didn't want to have anything to do with the person I was before. I wanted to construct a completely new identity for myself—one that didn't even like the same things I liked before."

She gapes at me in horror. "But you were so great back then!"

I incline my head to one side. She takes that as a signal that I don't want her touching me. She stops instantly.

"Does it bother you that I became a different person?" I ask. "You keep calling me Dylan. I'm not Dylan anymore. I'm not the same person." I shouldn't be talking to her like this. I sound a lot harsher than I feel.

"It isn't that," she stammers. "You're so.....so different now...."

"Is that a bad thing?"

"NO!" she cries way too loudly and immediately corrects herself. "Not at all! I just.....The person you were before meant so much to me—not that the person you are now isn't awesome, too.....It's just.....so hard to combine the two. I....." She gulps. "I can't just forget about Dylan. I loved him so much! I spent so many years wanting him back—and I don't believe that he's completely dead. You're still Dylan even if you're Carter, too." She shuts her eyes and shakes her head fast. "I'm not making any sense here. I'm sorry."

"Keep going," I tell her. "Go ahead and say it. I want to hear it."

"You....." She drags her eyes open and looks up at me with the same wide-eyed stare of shocked amazement—almost like she can't believe

I'm real. "The person that I see as Carter—you're so incredible like this……"

Without warning, she extends her other hand toward me and it comes to rest of my chest between my jacket lapels.

Her touch drifts through my T-shirt into the skin of my chest. She's touching me like that—the same way she's been touching my head—but now her hand migrates to my body.

That touch sends an electric charge through me. No one has ever touched me like this. No one has ever gotten close enough to touch me like this.

She stares at her own hand like she's just realizing what she's doing here. Her pupils dilate when she feels my heart pounding through my T-shirt.

Her lips sag open in a little silent moan of desire. Her hand glides sideways across my chest, under my jacket, and down toward my ribs.

Her face flushes with so much obvious passion. I turn her on. I drive her wild the same way she drives me wild.

I sit frozen to the couch feeling her touching me. I can't move. My every nerve sizzles from the electricity pumping through me right now.

She lets out a little gasp of blatant raw ravenous hunger when she slides her hand down to my pecs where my nipples would be if I still had them.

Then she strokes back to the other side of my chest underneath my jacket. She runs her hand down to my ribs on that side….and her haunted, glazed eyes drift up to meet mine.

She stares into my eyes with such a look of pure carnal passion that I can't stand it. She's barely holding herself together. Her body is about to snap from all the energy and power coursing through her veins right now.

"What does your skin feel like?" she whispers under her breath.

"Hard," I tell her. "It feels hard and insensitive like a layer of armor. It doesn't feel the same as normal skin. It doesn't have the same nerve-endings."

She looks back down at her hand and watches it in a hypnotic trance as she follows my sternum up to my neck.

She traces my neck up to my throat, my ears, my scalp, and my cheeks. "Can you feel this?" she whispers.

"Yes, I can feel it."

Watching her fascinates me—and ignites my own passion beyond anything I ever thought possible. I want to take her, but watching her like this gives me such a thrill that I can't bring myself to stop her.

She goes back down to my chest and strokes me back and forth under my jacket. She goes into another trance watching her own hand touch me through my shirt.

"I want to touch you," she whispers. "I want to touch your skin." She glances up. "Does this bother you?"

"No, it doesn't bother me. If you want to touch me, you can."

I lean forward, pull off my jacket, and yank my shirt off over my head. I want her to touch me as much as she wants to. I would strip off naked, but something tells me that isn't what she means.

I lean back on the couch. Her face takes on an even more stunned, startled, amazed glow when she sees me with my shirt off.

She starts touching my bare skin on my chest, shoulders, down my arms, and every other part of me she can reach without taking my pants off. She can't touch my back, either, since I'm leaning against it.

The way she's looking at me pushes me over the edge. She's touching me like that. This is the first step. I'm going to do it with her. I have to. I can't live without her.

I bend in, kiss her once, and then pull her legs around me. I draw her into my lap so she straddles my waist.

Now she can touch me all she likes. Her body looks captivating in this position.

She doesn't notice at first when I touch her back through her dress. I stroke up her sides, down to her hips, and around to her magnificent ass arching away from my package.

She stares at my chest and shoulders for a while. Then she falls on me and gives me a huge, wet, blistering kiss right on the chest.

I practically yell out from the intensity of feeling her mouth on me. I gasp and then start panting in tormented agony as she moves her mouth across my chest kissing me again and again.

She crawls down to my sternum and across toward my shoulders. The heat and wetness of her kisses skyrocket me out of my mind.

My hand flies to her head. I want to nail her right now, but she's enjoying herself too much making me feel amazing.

She works her way up my neck and back to my mouth. When she finally gets there, she attacks me in brutal kisses.

Her hands won't stop touching me all over my chest, stomach, shoulders, neck, and head. She can't control herself.

She responds to every caress and squeeze I deliver to that mind-blowing body of hers. I crush her ass in one hand, pull her hips down hard against my swollen package, and she moans in ecstasy when I massage her breasts through her dress.

She goes ballistic when I slide my hands up her thighs, but I don't push her dress up. I want to. I'm bursting to get my hands on this tight little body of hers.

She doesn't slow down and she won't stop kissing me. She kisses me faster and harder and throws herself into every squeeze and manipulation. She moans for it and grinds against my crotch in blatant lust.

I have to take a fistful of her hair to pull her away from my mouth. "We don't have to do this," I tell her between ragged breaths.

"I want to!" she pants and lunges in to attack my mouth again. Just as fast, she breaks off and frowns at me. "Do you not want to? We don't have to if you don't want to."

"I do want to." I can't stop touching her. "I just....I've never done it with anyone. I might not be good enough for you."

She sits up straight, gazes down into my eyes with all that glazed wonder and awe, and her hands come to rest on my chest.

"I want to be your first!" she tells me...and then casts her eyes down. "I wish you could be my first. I regret that now."

"You couldn't know we would meet again like this." I cup her chin to make her look up at me. "Are you sure you're okay with this—with doing it with someone who doesn't know what he's doing?"

"You do know what you're doing." She seems to come to some decision and straightens up a little more. "I want to. I want to be your first. I want to be the first person to taste you like this....."

She sinks into my neck, kisses me with her mouth wide open, and inches back down to my chest.

Her kisses burn into me creeping lower and lower. I can't breathe when her scorching hot mouth drags across my stomach and down.

I try to get my pants open fast enough before I explode, but she takes hold of them first.

She pulls them open and my straining, pulsing shaft falls into her greedy mouth.

I collapse back on the couch and feel her swallowing me. In that moment, I know the truth without her telling me.

She doesn't want the boy I used to be. She could never touch Dylan like this or give him the greatest pleasure of his life. Dylan was only her friend.

The person she wants is Carter. The way she's been looking at me—the way she touches my skin with such wonder and amazement—the way she inhales my body into her and consumes the brutal outpouring of all my explosive passion—she wants me the way I am now.

I'm good enough for her. I'm more than good enough. She can't get enough of me.

Chapter 18:
Sophie

I tense in pure raw rapture as Carter tightens his fist in my hair and pushes my head down on his throbbing shaft.

"Holy shit, baby!" he gasps. "Oh, yeah! Oh, my God! Yes!"

He arches back on the couch, thrusts into my mouth, and his whole body tenses before he unloads into my mouth. He bares his teeth, clamps his eyes shut, and gives one brutal shudder before he wilts onto the couch.

He doesn't think to loosen his fingers before he buckles shaking and spasming in front of me.

I untangle my hair from his hands and sit back to admire him. He looks so unbelievably strong and powerful like this. He lies in front of me with his shirt off and the lamplight glowing on his scars.

I can't help but touch him even though he keeps his eyes closed.

I don't care if that's as far as we go tonight. I just want to give him the pleasure he deserves. I want to be the first woman to give him that.

I sit back on my heels, but before I can even put my hands on his chest again, he snaps awake, sits up, and scoops me back onto his lap.

He lifts me by my armpits and steers my thighs onto either side of his lap. He's limp now, so him having his fly hanging open doesn't mean anything.

He comes back to full awareness in a split second. If I thought he was in any danger of slowing down, he proves me drastically wrong.

He cradles the back of my head and steers my mouth to his. He attacks my lips so much harder than before. Satisfying him only makes him more ravenous and demanding.

His hands range all over my body the way he did before, but he isn't slowing down this time.

His fingertips dig into my spine and then he grabs my ass to pull me tight into his hips. He sneaks his fingers a little farther behind me toward the slit between my thighs, but he pulls away when he hears me squeal in excitement.

He massages his hands up my thighs getting dangerously close to my crotch. He massages my breasts while his lips and tongue consume my mouth to eternity.

All these little movements add up to a torrential cascade of unstoppable passion. I want him to go all the way. I want him to put me out of my misery, but as insistent and demanding as he acts, he still doesn't take it further.

He keeps going through the same combination of maddening, teasing movements until I sob in molten desire. Can he feel how soaking wet my panties are right now?

He brings his hands up to cradle my cheeks in both his warm, strong palms. He kisses me gently...tenderly....

I don't want him to treat me gently or tenderly. I want him to consume me and ruin me.

Just when I think I might lose my mind entirely, he drags his mouth off my lips, crawls down my neck, and his powerful fingertips rake my sleeves off my shoulders.

He takes my bra straps with them and I shiver all over when I realize what he's doing.

I sob in ecstasy when he pulls my dress and bra down. My breasts fall out into his face and he doesn't hold back this time.

He flattens one hand against my back to crush me into his hungry mouth. He sucks my nipples in hard one after another while his other hand crushes, squeezes, pinches, and teases me to screaming madness.

I struggle against all this mind-blowing energy coursing through me. He's taking me there the same way he took me in his truck.

I want to get away from the feeling that I'm about to blast apart into a million pieces, but I only wind up throwing myself harder into his mouth.

He lets go of my breasts, but only with his hand. He continues devouring them while he scrapes both hands up my thighs, pushes my dress up to my hips, and glides underneath it to my panties.

He fingers around the edges, back to my ass, and finally feels how blisteringly wet I am. I can't contain this much longer.

I try to push myself onto his fingers, but he holds off. He squeezes me through my panties from behind, gives me a quick, tempting circular rub, and before I know what's happening, he thrusts his fingers all the way in.

I scream as a spike of rapture hits me. I thrust myself down on his fingers and rocket into another earth-shattering climax.

He tightens his grip on me, flattens his other hand against my spine, and forces my chest into his mouth while he crams his fingers to the limit.

His mouth blasts my skin to smithereens. I have no choice but to arch my chest into his mouth so he can demolish my breasts in big, brutal mouthfuls.

I hurl myself down on his fingers screaming to the skies—and just as fast, he pulls his fingers out and slips his rock-hard shaft into place instead.

I crumble in his hands, but he doesn't let me go. He holds me in exactly the same position and drives to the hilt. How did he get so hard again so fast?

He releases my breasts from his mouth, but that hardly helps me. My body takes on a mind of its own plowing into his thrusts, but he's already sitting up on the edge of the couch to drill me to the ends of the Earth.

He looks up at me. I think he wants to kiss me, but just as fast, his fingers thread into my hair from behind, pulls my head back, and force me to arch backward again.

My breasts stick in his face, but he doesn't attack them the way he did before. He holds me like that slamming his wicked spike into me again and again.

He holds me in the one position that will make me scream the loudest. Nothing will muffle those screams.

My voice breaks as the agony of all these fireworks explode through me. I thrash in his arms, but my own movements only seem to hurl me down on him even harder.

He dives in to bite my neck and then my shoulders, but all those sensations get lost in the magnificence of this moment.

He wraps his powerful arm around my waist to pound me in time to his rhythm. He arches his hips up to destroy me with each masterful thrust.

I'm just about to completely collapse in a ragged puddle of bliss when he eases off. He doesn't wait for me to stop sobbing and whimpering in rapture.

He pulls his fingers loose from my hair and pushes me off him while I'm still quivering and spasming from so many internal explosions.

He pushes me off his lap and has to hold me steady while I catch my balance. I can't think clearly enough to understand what he wants to do.

He stands me up in front of him while he still sits on the couch. Then he very slowly pulls my dress down the rest of the way off my arms and slides it past my hips to my feet.

He pulls off my bra and panties at the same time until I stand naked in front of him.

He bends over so I can step out of the dress, lays everything aside, and before I can even think, he scoops up two handfuls of my ass and brings my fragrant, trembling flesh to his mouth.

I burst into loud, keening sobs as his mouth lights me on fire. I can barely hold myself up, but he steadies me by crushing both my ass cheeks in his hands.

I buckle in another torturous orgasm as his tongue finds its way all the way inside my flaming slit.

He doesn't stop until he teases me to another short, quick, crushing orgasm. I can't stand this. I can't survive him taking me and owning me like this.

He keeps going this time until my screams break down in pathetic whimpering moans.

He leans back, but he doesn't straighten up. He keeps delivering quick, light licks every now and then to my swollen lips. Each of those torturous teasing licks sends me reeling back into the clouds of ecstasy.

He doesn't stop when he works his fingers between my thighs and buries them inside me in another powerful thrust.

I scream and almost fall over before he grabs me with one muscular arm around my waist.

He grips me hard around the waist, teases my clit to raging agony, and plunges his fingers deep inside me again and again until he makes me scream.

I shudder and buck in his arms. I claw at his shoulder trying to cope with all this bliss he's giving me.

I lose track of how long he keeps doing it. I can't think. I can't even be sure anymore that I exist.

I feel myself falling, but when I swim back to my senses, I'm still standing up—or he's holding me up. I can't feel my legs well enough to tell.

Chapter 19: Sophie

I almost fall over again the minute Carter lets me go and sits back on the couch.

I can't stop moaning. Explosive rocket blasts of ecstasy and brutal pleasure make me twitch and spasm every few seconds.

He takes hold of me and steers me down on his lap—sitting sideways this time.

I crumble in his arms. My head falls on his shoulder and I sob and whimper in tortured satisfaction. I can't believe he's doing this to me.

He kisses me on the head and cradles me in his arm, but only for a second before he starts touching me again.

He strokes down my arm to my hip and then slides his hand up between my thighs again. He doesn't give me an instant to rest before he starts driving me to the stars again.

I spasm back against his arm and he lets me jolt. My body goes rigid, but he doesn't stop. He lets me lie back just enough so he can see me thrashing and contorting on his fingers.

He stares down at me with brutal intensity. That's the moment when I realize. He only did it with me once. He doesn't act like he wants to do it again.

He's enjoying watching me. He's doing this so he can see me fall apart in front of him. He wants to see that he can take me to the stars again.....and again.....and again.

I burst into another fit of ragged screaming when I realize the awful truth. I'm putty in his hands. I can't resist him. If he wants to watch me shatter into a million screaming orgasms, I can only succumb to the demands of his fingers, hands, mouth, and body.

I don't want to be anywhere else. I ached for this so badly. Now he's turning out to be something so much more than I bargained for.

He won't let me go until he wrings me of every drop of passion he can squeeze from my body. He wants it all.

Just in case I thought I was doing it with kind, gentle, soft-spoken Dylan, I only have to open my eyes to see exactly who is doing this to me.

Carter is determined and unstoppable. He's already seen the worst. Now he wants the best and he wants it all. He won't stop until he gets exactly what he wants.

I don't want him to stop. I want him to own my body and make it his own.

I wanted to be his first and now I am. I'm the vehicle that allows him to make up for all these years alone.

In a way, he's been saving himself for this moment. No one else deserved him. I can't believe my good luck that I get to be the one who receives this power of his.

I just don't know how I can survive all these brutal orgasms. My mind is already gone. My body flies completely out of control, but that's okay because he's in control of everything I do.

He slips his fingers out of me and leaves me gasping, panting, moaning, and trembling in his arms.

He sucks my juices off his fingers and lifts me up to cradle me against his shoulder again.

He hugs me there, kisses me on the forehead, and lets me wrap my arms around his neck for whatever protection I can get before he takes me to the limit again.

I know he will. He didn't satisfy himself when he did it with me just now.

I don't know what will satisfy him. Maybe nothing will. Maybe he'll just keep going forever and I'll never be able to keep up with him.

I whimper against his neck just praying he won't let me go. I couldn't stand it if he told me he was done for the night. I need him too much. I know that now.

I need him to get me through this. I need to hold onto him from the storm that is both of us.

He keeps kissing me on the forehead and running his fingers through my hair. I start trembling all over as the energy leaves me. I don't know what to do with myself. I couldn't function right now if I wanted to.

He clamps his arms around me to steady me, but the trembling doesn't stop. I want to beg him for help, but I can't form words right now.

Almost as if he reads my mind, he stands up, lifts me in his arms, and walks away through the apartment to his bedroom.

He angles sideways to carry me into it, sits down on the edge of the bed to kick off his shoes, and then scoots around to lay me on the bed. I don't want to let go of him. I want to hide in him.

He crawls onto the bed next to me, tries to kiss me, and then props himself on his elbow next to me.

He stares down at me from above while he traces his fingertips from my face to my chest and back to the throbbing slit between my legs.

I try to kiss him and fail before I scream again. I completely fall apart when he drives his fingers in and makes me climax again....and again.....and again.....

I scream my loudest hanging onto him for dear life, but the more out of control I fall, the more it seems to satisfy him. He just doesn't stop.

I buck against his hand to take him so much deeper than he thrusts into me. My juices cover his hand and flow down my ass to stain my thighs. Will it ever end?

When he finally finishes, I wilt into the bed, completely spent. I couldn't move right now if my life depended on it.

I'm just floating into outer space when Carter crawls into my arms again and starts kissing me. I can finally think clearly enough to kiss him back.

I fold my arms around his neck and submerge into the heat of his skin next to mine. He feels so strong and hard and powerful. His body sinks against me.....and I feel that he isn't wearing his jeans anymore.

That blaze of heat translates all the way down to his legs. His bare thighs graze mine when he slips his knee between my legs. He pushes my thighs apart....and eases on top of me between my legs.

I'm so rubbery and melted by so many orgasms that my flesh offers no resistance. He glides inside me on a river of wetness.

My muscles clamp around his shaft in a death grip as internal spasms ripple up and down his rigid slab. Holy crap, he feels so damn good!

He doesn't stop kissing me as he pushes my legs apart and starts drilling into me much more slowly than before. Can he feel how lush and hungry my body is for every torturous inch of him?

He breaks off my mouth, pushes himself up on his arms, and arches into me in slow, cruel, spiraling thrusts.

"Look at me, baby!" he whispers. "Open your eyes and look at me."

My eyes float open in a haze of rapture. I feast my eyes on his haunted, mangled appearance.

He looms over me like some kind of apparition—or maybe a ghost of some forgotten natural force. He doesn't look human like this. He looks like an almighty supernatural being who can command mortal flesh to respond to everything he does.

His shoulders swell with muscle when he pushes himself up for each stroke. He towers over me holding me enthralled with those all-seeing eyes.

My body responds to him exactly the way he wants me to. I feel myself rising to another crushing climax. My body responds to every inch of his smoking meat exactly the way I responded to his fingers.

He gasps with the intensity of each thrust. His features wrench and he bares his teeth. That expression transforms him into something even more foreign and otherworldly. I can't get enough of seeing him like this.

I drift away into the fantasy that he's some kind of demigod or force of nature come to Earth to take me to places I would never be able to go by myself.

I teeter on the brink of another massive collapse when, without warning, he rolls sideways onto his back. He pulls me on top of him and draws my thighs on either side of his hips so I straddle him again.

That position blasts me the rest of the way out of my mind and I pump into him with all my might. I scream out, arch back, and then sit up the rest of the way to ride him to eternity.

Chapter 20: Carter

I wake up with my face buried in Sophie's plush, soft breasts. I nuzzle closer and turn my greedy mouth into them to suck.

I tighten my arms around her waist to hold her there against me. I don't want this to end. I want to disappear into the heavenly feeling of these magical pillows surrounding both sides of my face.

She sighs in her sleep and her arms close around my head to hug me into her. She pulls me closer and then yelps when I start sucking her nipples.

She arches her back and her breasts thrust deeper into my face exactly where I want them.

She fell asleep with her thighs wrapped around my waist and one leg thrown over my hips. Her blissful, fragrant juices still cover my shaft. Her smell drifts into my nose when I turn over to face her.

She doesn't open her eyes. Her face goes slack in sleep and her hair spills over her eyes to hide her features.

She intoxicates me like this. I can't believe I got so lucky as to spend the greatest night of my life with this angel.

Now she softens in my arms and her magnificent breasts fall into my mouth while I slot between her legs.

My shaft glides home into a forgotten galaxy of hot wetness. She surrounds me in velvety softness as her muscles clench around me. She feels absolutely sublime.

She whines and then moans out loud when I start to thrust. I could take her all day and for another night. I never want to stop.

Doing it with her gives me unstoppable energy. Just lying next to her and fingering her to make her scream and writhe on my hand—it's beyond magical.

I absolutely love watching her orgasm. I've never seen anything more beautiful and enthralling. I want to keep playing with her body for the rest of my life and just watch her orgasm again....and again.... and again.

I really don't care if I ever get off again. I don't need to—but here I am inside her.

She orgasms like that on my shaft just as easily. She pushes herself against me to take it all the way in.

She undulates on the bed next to me and hugs my head tighter against her breasts the faster I thrust into her. Her yelps and squeals rise to full-throated screams.

I love making her scream like that. I love watching her fall apart knowing I took her there. I want to shatter her into a million pieces and feel her clinging to me for safety afterward so I can do it all over again.

I rear back so I can get a better look at her face when she climaxes. She changes so rapidly between clamping her eyes shut, grimacing in torment, and then staring at me in shocked astonishment before going through the cycle again.

As soon as I pull away from her, she arches downward and plants her hands on the mattress to support herself, now that I'm not there to hold her in position.

That one movement changes the whole dynamic between us. Her hair falls forward to curtain her face. She pants faster and tilts her hips backward to take my thrusts from a different angle.

I want to take her like that. I want to conquer her like that at least once.

I rotate onto my knees thinking she might roll onto her back, but she stays on her side. I wind up straddling her legs and drilling into her from below.

She doesn't fight me. In fact, she bends her spine and ass all the way back to take me in the most animalistic way possible.

I bend over her husking and growling in her ear. Her rising whines turn back into screams until, in one moment of sheer abandon, she tosses her hair back and glances at me over her shoulder.

She thrusts back on me and snarls at me taking it all the way in before her face spasms in another orgasm.

She bursts into the same screams I've been hearing all night long. Seeing and hearing her like this blasts me out of my mind and I can't hold back.

I topple onto her from behind as my whole being unloads into her. I crush her in my arms feeling torturous waves of completion pump deep inside her burning flesh.

I collapse on top of her husking in her ear. She keeps whimpering and shuddering in time to her inner muscles rippling and flowing down my shaft every few seconds.

She buckles underneath me and doesn't try to fight her way out of my arms. She sinks into a fevered haze.

The smell coming from her hair, skin, and flesh blurs my conscious mind. I reel in drunken ecstasy on everything she is. I don't want to be anywhere else but right here next to her.

All good things must come to an end, though. I'm just starting to drift into the stratosphere when the alarm goes off on my phone.

I groan and roll off her, but she doesn't move. I have to fish around in my pants to find the phone so I can turn off my alarm.

I throw the phone onto the bedroom chair and flop back onto the bed so I can savor these last few seconds of blissful intoxication before I have to get up and function.

I shut my eyes and feel the velvet caress of Sophie's hands, breasts, hair, and body covering me.

She strokes my skin, kisses me all over, and climbs on top of me before she starts crawling her way down between my legs again.

"Don't, baby...." I groan. "Please....."

She mumbles something as she nuzzles into my shaft. I feel myself starting to get hard and she takes me in her mouth.

I barely manage to say, "Baby...." again. I raise my hand to stop her, but I only wind up taking hold of her head as she starts to suck harder.

Now it's my turn to whimper in agony. She's going to suck the life out of me if I don't do something to stop this—but I can't stop it.

She sucks faster and sinks deeper onto me. Her hot, wicked tongue flashes around my shaft and teases my balls each time she goes down on me.

I groan and then start roaring as she brings me back to another crushing explosion.

I grab her head and unload into her mouth. I can't even yell at her how good that feels.

She leaves me completely wrecked on the bed. How the hell am I supposed to function today?

We both have to go to work. Sweet Jesus, how am I going to get through that when she's working right in front of me?

How do all these married men handle themselves so professionally? How do they not grab their wives and bend them over right there in the middle of the firehouse? I really don't understand it.

Sophie crawls up my body, torments me by dragging her breasts over my still twitching shaft and up my stomach, and lays her glorious self on top of me to start kissing me.

I have to act now before she seduces me into taking her again.

I don't allow myself to feel how deliciously soft, malleable, and seductive she feels when I put my arms around her.

I flip her over and throw her down on her back on the bed. "Stop it, baby," I tell her. "Stop playing around. We both need to go to work today."

She smirks at me and spreads both thighs to stroke me with her legs. "I know," she drawls in her sultriest tone. "I'm going to be quivering for you all day watching you telling everyone what to do and giving orders all over the firehouse."

I can't look at her glorious body stretched out all naked in front of me. "Go take a shower—now."

She winces and gasps in mock excitement. "Ooo! I love it when you get all commanding and demanding. Make me your obedient servant—please."

"I told you to stop it." I have to stop this before I fall for her temptation. "Go get in the shower so I can drive you home before your shift."

She climbs out of bed, but she looks even more magnificent sauntering across my bedroom stark naked.

She grins at me over her shoulder. "Are you sure you don't want to come and join me?"

"I'm sure I do—which is why I won't. I'll wait until you get out."

She laughs and goes into the bathroom attached to my bedroom. She calls out to me while she turns on the water. "Just remember you still owe me dinner from last night. I'm putting it on your tab."

"I gave you dinner—and breakfast this morning," I tease. "You just had it."

She bursts out laughing. Her high, musical voice echoes off the bathroom tiles and makes my stomach twist in knots.

I have to seriously stop myself from going in there, pushing her against the tiles, and giving her another dose right now.

Chapter 21:
Carter

I pick up my phone to distract myself from seeing Sophie's naked body disappear into my bathroom.

I find a whole bunch of emails waiting for me from my supervisor at the State Health and Safety Commission. He's already sending me the details of my next posting after I finish auditing Howe Firehouse.

What am I going to do about that? I have to figure out what to do about Sophie—and everything else.

I can't have a relationship with her as long as I'm her superior officer—and I'll always be her superior officer as long as I'm the Health and Safety auditor for Howe Firehouse.

I'll still be her superior officer even after I finish this audit. I always will be as long as I still do this job.

So that leaves me with only two options. I can either quit my job and have a relationship with her or I can keep my job and leave her.

I would never ask her to give up her job. I couldn't do that to her—and I don't want to give up my job, either. I worked hard to get where I am.

Wouldn't it be worth it to have a relationship with her—with the woman of my dreams? It's just a job. I can get another job anywhere.

I can't think about that right now. I go out to the kitchen and start making breakfast until I hear Sophie come out of the bathroom.

I manage to dodge her and avoid her predatory clutches before I slip into the bathroom behind her and shut the door in her face. I hear her laughing before the spray hits my head and drowns out the sound.

I get out of the shower to find breakfast waiting for me. She will not stop smirking at me through the whole meal.

"Please tell me you aren't going to be smiling at me like that at work today," I tell her. "You'll give the whole show away."

She blushes and laughs. "I'll behave. I promise."

I snort. "Yeah, right. Tell me another one."

She smirks at me again. "I have to get it out now while I can. You can't blame me for being happy about last night—and this morning."

"I'm not blaming you for anything. Last night was incredible."

She looks up at me. Her skin and eyes glow. "Really? It didn't disappoint your adolescent fantasies?"

"Cut it out—and no, it didn't. It beat them."

She bursts into a huge blushing grin. "Yay! I'm so glad."

I have to ease close to her, slip my arm around her waist, and kiss her, but I make sure to do it gently so I don't wind up starting something again.

"You're everything I ever dreamed you would be and more," I murmur. "Thank you. I can die contented now."

"No, you can not!" She pulls away, pretends to swat at me, and grins again. "We're going to do it again! I insist."

I have to laugh. "Yes, Ma'am. As you wish."

"Damn straight." She downs the rest of her coffee and her expression goes serious when she glances around my apartment.

She has no choice but to wear the same dress from last night. It doesn't look as dressy in the light of day. Now it just looks casual and girl-next-door charming.

She picks up my blazer from the floor next to the couch. "Would you mind if I wear this—just on the way home?"

"Sure. Whatever you want. Why do you want to? You look beautiful the way you are."

She blushes at me while she pulls the blazer on. "I wouldn't want to look like this for anyone but you."

She flips her hair across the back of the jacket and pulls the sleeves up to her elbows.

The blazer is too big for her in the shoulders, but it still completes a totally different look. She doesn't look as stunningly attractive like this. She still looks casual, but more understated.

I finish putting on my uniform, escort her out to my truck, and drive her home. She kisses me long and deep in the driveway. "Thank you for last night," she whispers. "I can't wait to do it again."

"You're so sweet," I tell her. "I'll be dreaming about you until then."

She kisses me one more time and again after I let her out of the passenger seat. "Bye," she murmurs.

"Bye," I reply. "Have a good day at work, okay?"

"I will because you'll be there." She flashes me another grin and races inside.

I have to stop myself from thinking about her on the way to the firehouse. Then I have to concentrate not to notice her when she eventually shows up for work.

I go through a confused turmoil of colliding worldviews when I see that tight, curvy body in a Fire Department uniform.

I admired her figure when I first showed up here. Now I know more than I ever wanted to know about the body underneath.

That isn't true. I don't know nearly enough about it. She's right. I can't wait to get my hands on her again. Just don't ask me how I'm going to do that when we have to work together like this.

She stays out of my way while I deal with a bunch of new problems. Danny shows up on crutches with a brace around his leg after tearing the ligaments in his knee at the convenience store the other night.

He's wearing casual clothes, which means the roster will continue to be a problem. I spend an hour with Chief Brewer in his office trying to come up with some solution to his continuous staffing shortages.

He can only fill all the necessary shifts by rostering me in place of his regular firefighters and paramedics. I'm not supposed to work regular shifts. I'm supposed to ride along with the regular crew and observe, but it just isn't working out that way.

We go downstairs at eleven o'clock. I've succeeded in avoiding Sophie all morning. Now I can't avoid her anymore.

We find the crew in the training room for our next Health and Safety briefing. The second shift is also there in their casual clothes. This is a mandatory meeting, so everyone has to attend.

Sophie sits on one side of the room with Naomi, Jessie, and Brooke. I can somewhat pretend Sophie isn't there and concentrate on the rest of the crew.

Danny lays his crutches on the ground and props his leg brace out in front of him. He's Exhibit A for the talk I'm going to give this morning.

"Welcome back to our next Health and Safety meeting," I begin. "Today we're going to go over the accident that happened at the convenience store and figure out where we could have done better to prevent the injuries that resulted from the...."

"No way are you pinning this one on me!" Andy blurts out. "I knew you were going to pull something like this! What happened was not my fault!"

I look up in what I hope looks like surprise, but I'm not surprised. I wouldn't be surprised even if Chief Brewer hadn't warned me about this.

"I never said what happened was your fault," I tell Andy. "The fact remains that both the patient and Danny got hurt as a result of preventable...."

"You see?!" Andy shoots out an accusing finger and points at me. "You all heard him! He's manipulating what happened to make it out that I did something wrong! Go on. Tell everyone how I screwed up and caused the whole mess because I didn't secure the oxygen tank." He sits back and crosses his arms over his chest. "I'm waiting."

"I never said you did anything wrong," I insist in as calm a voice as I can muster. "I was standing right there and I saw as clearly as everyone else that you couldn't secure the oxygen tank because the MAST suit took up too much space on the gurney. Even Chief Brewer was there. Anyway, even if you did put the oxygen tank on the gurney, something could have failed or the cop could have knocked the gurney over and then the tank could have exploded the MAST suit, too. Then the patient would have been in even more trouble...."

He doesn't wait for me to finish. He shoots to his feet and points at me. "You know what? I smelled a rat when you first came to work here and now we're all seeing it! You're pinning this on me so you can drive a wedge between me and Sophie."

My jaw drops. "You can't be serious!"

"Pull your head in, man," Keith growls from across the room. "Carter was never going to pin that accident on you. It was the cop's fault if it was anyone's. Just cool your jets, sit down, and hear him out."

"Yeah," Danny calls over his shoulder. "Accidents happen to the best of us. The patient would have been fine if that cop hadn't slipped. We all saw that."

Andy doesn't hear either of them. "This asshole has been a cancer in this department ever since he first showed his face here. He gave us this big sob story about how he got caught in a fire so we won't see what a snake he is. Now he's trying to twist this whole audit against us "

"That's enough, Andy," Chief Brewer snaps. "I'm giving you five seconds to sit down and shut up. If you don't, you'll be suspended without pay."

Andy ignores him completely. "I'm going to file a formal complaint against you with the Health and Safety Commission for inappropriate conduct. They'll investigate you and prove that I'm right." He turns on Chief Brewer with a vicious sneer. "If you suspend me without pay for blowing the whistle on this creep, you'll wind up in the hot seat, too."

Andy storms out with those words ringing in the air.

Chapter 22: Carter

I pause at the top of the stairs—just long enough to hear the rest of the crew laughing and joking around down in the garage.

God only knows how I got through the rest of the Health and Safety briefing after Andy threatened me with a formal complaint. If he really does bring up my relationship with Sophie, I'm screwed.

Andy can't bring it up because no one knows about my relationship with Sophie. No one even knows I went out with her last night. No one knows she spent the night at my apartment.

No one in the whole fire crew even knows about her childhood friend Dylan or how it affected her. She never talked to anyone about it. She said so herself.

No one on the crew can connect me to her that way, either. Andy doesn't have a leg to stand on, but if he really does file this complaint, then I can never see her again. I probably couldn't even see her casually at firehouse events—not without raising suspicion.

I really need to talk to her about it, but I can't do that here.

I shake that off and continue down the hall to Chief Brewer's office. This one promises to be a much more difficult confrontation.

He looks up when I walk in. "Hey, man," he tells me. "Come on in and shut the door."

I shut it. Christ knows I don't want anyone else hearing this.

He doesn't ask me to take a seat, thank God. I stand in front of his desk. I'm his superior officer or at least equal to him in rank, but I've never felt more like a raw recruit.

He leans back in his chair and rotates it from side to side. "It turns out that Andy hasn't wasted any time on following through on his threat. He already filed the complaint before he even made that announcement at the meeting. He must have been planning this since he first confronted you about Sophie."

I compress my lips. "Thanks for telling me."

He swings his chair around to study me head-on. "I have to ask this. Is there anything going on between you and Sophie?"

I don't even hesitate before I say, "Yes."

He only nods. "What are you going to do about that?"

"How the hell should I know?" I shut my mouth real quick. I shouldn't be swearing in front of him.

He pretends to check his computer. "I have no choice but to take you off duty as our Health and Safety officer until we hear the outcome of this complaint. You know that, right?"

I dip my chin once. "Yeah, I know."

"I would like to ask you, as a favor to me and the rest of the crew, if you wouldn't mind staying on as a firefighter-paramedic. We need you too badly. I'll roster you on opposite shifts from Andy as much as I can. I'll do my absolute best to make it so you never have to see him again—but I can't promise that you won't get rostered on with him sometime. Just....please.....please stay. I can't run this place without you
."

I compress my lips again. This is the absolute last situation in the world that I want to be in right now.

"Fine," I snap. "I'll do it for you and the crew and the patients."

He bows his head. "Thank you. You don't know how grateful I am."

I wait for him to indicate that the interview is over. That bastard Andy finally got what he wanted. He got me busted down to a grunt firefighter.

Too bad he didn't succeed in actually getting rid of me. In a way, he's stuck with me because of his complaint.

Chief Brewer studies me for a second. I stand in front of him seething with buried rage—and something else.

He finally stands up, walks around his desk, and sits down on the edge of it in front of me so he has to look up at me. "Are you gonna be okay, man? You're one of the best paramedics I've ever met. We're all honored to have you with us. I'm sure Sophie feels the same way. You can't let one bad apple ruin this for you—but you have to understand that my hands are tied. He backed me into a corner with this complaint. If I try to discipline him now, he'll say I'm retaliating against a whistleblower."

I can't look at him, so I turn my head away. "I should have known this was going to happen."

"Why? Has it happened before?"

"It isn't that," I mumble. "I should have known something would go wrong. I never should have started anything with Sophie. I knew it couldn't work out and now everything else is messed up because of it. I never should have let it happen. I was a chump for thinking I could ever be happy." I glance at him. "Are we done here? I need to get back to work."

"Yeah, man. We're done. Thank you again for staying on. I really appreciate it."

I only nod and turn away. I hate everything about this.

"Carter!" he calls after me.

I glance over my shoulder at him. The sympathy and understanding in his eyes twist a knife in my guts.

He walks over to the door, stops in front of me, and lowers his voice. "Listen to me, man. This complaint—it could be a blessing in disguise. Don't you see? You aren't Sophie's superior officer anymore. There's no more reason you two can't be together. The complaint could turn out to be the best thing for both of you."

I stare at the floor taking that in. Wasn't I just thinking I would have to quit my job to ever have a relationship with her?

I didn't have to quit my job. I just had to get suspended from it.

I was also just thinking that now Andy is stuck with me because of this complaint. What if Chief Brewer is right?

I still have a job—and I still have Sophie.

I go downstairs. All the firefighters and paramedics are still goofing around in the garage. I'm just about to look around to see where Andy is when I get a message from my supervisor at the State Health and Safety Commission.

He's extremely apologetic and supportive. He tells me he's already spoken to Chief Brewer about the whole thing.

My supervisor tells me he knows I wouldn't do anything like what Andy is claiming in his complaint, but the Commission's hands are tied just like Chief Brewer's are.

They have no choice but to take me off the Howe audit until they can gather enough proof to dismiss the complaint.

He says it shouldn't take long. He can see that Andy's complaint is thin on the details.

Chief Brewer has already backed me up and given the Commission a dozen names of my coworkers who can vouch for me. This crew really is something special.

Chief Brewer has also told my supervisor about me staying on as a firefighter-paramedic to help fill the gaps in the Howe roster. My supervisor gives me his blessing and tells me to enjoy myself before I come back on the job.

I make a snap decision. I wasn't planning to, but it just comes out n the spur of the moment.

I message my supervisor back and tell him that this incident is making me realize I don't want to be a Health and Safety inspector anymore. I just want to work in the field like I used to.

I tell him I don't want to continue in this role. I'm committed to finishing the Howe audit once the Commission reinstates me, but I won't take another inspector job after this. I've decided to stay on at Howe indefinitely.

As soon as I type the words into my phone, I know it's right. Sophie is more important to me than the job—the inspector's job.

Being a firefighter and a paramedic has always been in my blood. I could never give that up and I don't have to.

I would have to give *her* up if I kept working for the Commission. I've dreamed of this for too long. I can't let her go again—not now when I just got her back.

My supervisor writes back and says he'll be sorry to see me go, but he understands and to let him know if anything changes and I ever want to come back on the job.

I thank him as politely as I can and put my phone away. Now I have to go through the rest of my shift dealing with Andy's giant attitude.

The minute I look up, I freeze again when I see Sophie confronting Andy across the garage floor. They stand next to the rescue truck while the rest of the crew stands around watching.

"What's this bullshit about you filing a complaint against Carter?" she demands.

He squirms and glances around at everyone staring at him. They glare in outright hatred. The guy sure does know how to make enemies. It's one of the very few things he's good at.

"I told you I was going to file a complaint," he mumbles. "What did you think—that I just said that to hear myself talk?"

"Yes!" she blurts out. "You said it just to hear yourself talk and to get attention and to make trouble for someone who's a thousand times' better paramedic than you are! We all know this complaint is a stunt, Andy! No one ever drove a wedge between us. You did that all by yourself!"

He tries to look away, but she's fuming so badly that he winds up watching her anyway. I don't blame him. She looks like she might attack him any second now.

Maybe that's why the rest of the crew is standing around watching, too—so they can pull her off when she tries to dive in and tear his head off.

I hang back by the stairs. I don't want to get involved in this.

I should. I should be the one to go over there and pull Sophie away from him. I don't want her defending me—except that I do.

Just then, Chief Brewer comes downstairs, takes the old roster off the bulletin board, pins up the new one, and happens to glance around enough to notice the confrontation escalating by the truck.

He only has to look once to see Sophie standing nose to nose with Andy. Chief Brewer is too smart not to know what it means.

He saunters over there like he's taking his kids to the park. "I just want you all to know that, pending the outcome of this complaint, Carter won't be working as our Health and Safety officer anymore. The Commission is suspending his status until they can clear up this matter."

Andy pumps his fist. "Yes! I knew he was rotten."

Chief Brewer levels him with a brutal glare. "You'll be happy to know that I've already given a statement in his favor. I've also given the Commission the names and contact details of seven other highly ranked members of our crew who will give statements that your complaint is totally without merit."

"You're damn right we will," Keith growls.

"If Carter is cleared, I'll be filing a counter-complaint against you for harassment and disability discrimination," Chief Brewer goes on. "I don't think I'll have any problem substantiating that complaint—which will result in you getting fired and probably banned from working anywhere in the medical field. I hope you're happy. Your own vindictive attitude is going to come back to bite you in the ass."

Andy's expression changes in a heartbeat. "You can't do this to me! I never did anything to him!"

"I don't know why you have such a beef against Carter, but we can all see that you've had it out for him since he first set foot in this firehouse," Chief Brewer goes on. "That doesn't matter, though, because you'll be happy to know that he's staying on here as a firefighter and a paramedic. I asked him to help us out with our roster since we're already shorthanded and now Danny is down, too."

The rest of the crew cheers, laughs, and slaps each other on the back. "Yeah! That's great!"

They look around for me so they can congratulate me. They see me standing by the stairs behind Chief Brewer.

I can't hang back anymore. I can't hide from this decision and I don't want to.

I take a few steps forward. "I want all of you to know that I resigned from my role as Health and Safety officer for the State Commission. I'll finish my audit on Howe Firehouse as soon as the commission reinstates me, but this will be my last Health and Safety audit. After that, I'll stay on here if you'll all have me."

More cheers break out. People start to mob around me. They grab me, squeeze my neck and shoulders, and shake me while they laugh.

Their beaming faces say it all. This is right. I belong here.

"I also want all of you to know that Sophie and I are together," I tell them as soon as the noise dies down. "I don't want any secrets between me and the rest of the crew. I'm staying on and we're going to be together from now on."

She squeals out loud, jumps at me, throws her arms around my neck, and kisses me on the cheek in front of everyone.

"Yay!" she cries. Then she turns around and laughs in Andy's face. "Ha ha! You brainless, clueless idiot! Do you hear that? Thank you so much for filing that complaint, you dipshit! You gave us the greatest gift I can think of. Now Carter and I can finally be together. This is all possible because of you. You can sit back, light up a fat one, and watch us ride off into the sunset thanks to you."

He glares at her in outright hatred. He claims to care about her, but he obviously can't stand her. "This isn't over," he growls.

"Oh, it's over," she counters. "It's very over." She rushes me and kisses me again. Then she goes back to jumping up and down, clapping her hands, and fielding congratulations from everyone.

The others all move in to surround me. They ask a million questions—none of which have anything to do with how Sophie and I wound up together so fast after we supposedly just met.

So many people crowd around that I don't see Andy. By the time everyone disperses back to their jobs, Andy is gone.

Chapter 23: Sophie

I come out of the firehouse and carry my backpack out to my car where I spot Carter getting into his truck. He glances left and right and then grins at me. "Hey, pretty lady. Can I give you a ride home?"

I blush at him. "Only if you're giving me a ride home to your place."

He throws his duffel back into the back seat, comes over to me, slips his arm around my waist, and kisses me right there in the parking lot.

"I have a better idea," he murmurs. "How about I give you a ride home to our place."

I squeal again, lunge for him, and throw my arms around him. "I can't wait! I'm so happy you're staying!"

He buries his face in my hair. "I couldn't walk away from you. You're all I've ever wanted. I would give up a lot more to have you."

I loosen my grip on him just enough to kiss him again. Tears of happiness sting my eyes when I look at him. "Are you okay—about the complaint and the suspension and everything?"

"I'm fine with it. This crew is the best. I don't want to lose that, either."

I sniff. I don't seem to be able to stop kissing him, but just then, Chris, Josh, and Vince all come out of the firehouse to get into their cars, too.

I lower myself to the ground and take my arms down, but it's too late. Our crewmates have already seen me and Carter together—like everyone doesn't already know.

Carter and I stand in awkward silence until everyone leaves, but we're standing too close for anyone to mistake what we're doing.

"Come back to my place tonight," he murmurs. "We can talk there."

"I'm still in my uniform.....and I have to work tomorrow," I tell him. "I need to get some stuff from my apartment."

"I have to work tomorrow, too, so why don't I follow you home? You can get your things and then we'll drive to my place. How does that sound?"

I can't stop beaming at him, but this one conversation changes our relationship all over again. We're doing this.

We're going to be together. Our conversation is changing into the everyday mundane logistics of who drives where, when, gets what stuff, and how it's all going to work.

He sees the look in my eyes, bends in, and gives me one quick kiss before he nods toward my car. "I'll follow you to your place and we'll take it from there."

He waits just long enough for me to get behind the wheel. I smile at him and wave through the passenger window before I start the motor.

I love it when I see him standing there in a protective posture. Everything about his presence in my life gives me an unimaginable thrill. I can't believe my luck. I got him and now we're going to be together!

I have to control myself so I can drive home. He returns to his truck and we pull out onto the road.

He follows me to my apartment complex and accompanies me inside.

I bustle around packing a bunch of stuff into a duffle bag. I keep on the uniform I'm currently wearing and pack two others along with my toiletries, makeup, and a few casual outfits.

I don't know how long I'll be staying at Carter's place. It could turn out to be indefinite. I sure hope it does.

If it does, I'll be able to do laundry there so I can rotate my uniforms.

I come out to the living room and find him staring at pictures of my family hanging on the wall in the kitchen.

"I'm really sorry to hear about your brother," he tells me. "He was a great guy. He always treated me well—and he seemed to understand that you and I would wind up together."

I look away. "He was genuinely sorry when you left. I think he might have been one of the very few people who realized how hard it hit me. He didn't say anything about you, but he tried to take extra good care of me after that. The problem was that he was so much older. He went to college at the end of that year, so he wasn't around much."

"That sucks," he murmurs. "It's a tragedy that you lost him so soon."

"I don't know that he could have done anything for me. I just wish he had a chance to live his life. I really miss him nowadays."

"I bet. I'm sorry you had to go through that." He shakes his head and turns around. "It just makes me wish I had been there for more of your life.....so we'll just have to make sure that never happens again."

I smile up at him and turn to the pile of notes and paperwork at the end of the counter. I have a few bills I still need to pay and other business to attend to.

I start folding up the paperwork to take it over to Carter's place, too. I'll deal with it there—if he ever lets me out of the bedroom.

Almost as if my thoughts make it happen, he comes up behind me, places both hands on my shoulders, and squeezes in a comforting, massaging motion.

The last twenty-four hours have taught me too much about his body. This isn't a comforting, massaging squeeze. It's the prelude to something more—a lot more.

His body sizzles with tension behind me, and before I know what's happening, he sinks his hot, hungry mouth into my neck from behind.

His hands slide down my shoulders to my sides. He follows the curve of my chest around the outsides of my breasts to my waist and down to my hips.

"Do you know how hot you are in that uniform?" he rasps in my ear. "Do you know how hard you make me went you bend over and stick out your ass for me to drool over?"

He pushes me forward against the kitchen counter and crams his swollen package against my ass from behind.

I gasp when I feel the brutal tension holding him just inside the breaking point. He gets so hard so fast. It comes out of nowhere and leaves no room to doubt—just like everything else he does.

His hands keep following my curves—around to my ass and up my back to my hair. He grabs my hips and pulls me back into his thrust at the same time that he pushes me harder against the counter.

He pushes one hand down flat on my spine to pin my breasts to the counter and husks under his breath. "You don't know how many times I've wanted to tear this uniform off you and have my way with you in the back of the locker room."

His low, strained voice sends a shiver up my spine. He's been fantasizing about me right there in the firehouse.

I try to remember how he acted when he first came to work at Howe Firehouse. He acted so professional then. No one would ever have known I meant anything to him.

He must have recognized me instantly. He might even have known I worked there before he started his audit.

What must he have been thinking and going through when I didn't recognize him?

He certainly is making up for it now. He keeps holding me down while he scoops his other hand up my thighs to my ass. He grabs me between the legs from behind and makes me squirm in an agony of desire.

I moan and try to struggle out of his hold, but that feeling of him holding me down only turns me on move. "Carter...." I moan.

"Mmmm, baby," he growls. "Give me that beautiful ass."

I try to push my ass back into his hand. His fingers between my legs make me want to climax right here, but he doesn't give me the chance.

He pushes his hand down between my shoulder blades a little harder to make sure I can't get away. Then he attacks my belt with his other hand, strips my pants open, and dives his fingers into my panties.

I yelp and then start to sob in ecstasy when he fingers me. I know I can orgasm like this, but he doesn't give me a chance to do that, either.

He pulls out and tugs my pants down to the middle of my thighs to expose my ass for his pleasure.

I can't separate my legs like this. I just have to lie here and seethe in desperation while he strokes my ass and murmurs to himself in clenched admiration of how fine my ass is.

He keeps grinding his throbbing package into me to drive me insane. "Please... Carter....." I moan. "Please.....take me......"

"Mmmmm, baby," he snarls. "I love it when you beg like that."

Hearing him talk like that pushes me to the breaking point. I want to burst into real tears when I realize he's just going to tease me like this. He doesn't really plan to take me against the kitchen counter.

I wish he would. I wish he would hold me down and ravage me because he knows I'm his to ravage.

He crushes my breast in one meaty hand and then follows the curve of my sides down to my hips again. He doesn't push up my shirt nor does he try to take it off to expose my breasts. He really wants to take me when I'm wearing my uniform. It really must turn him on.

Without a word of warning, he grabs both my arms just above the wrists, drops onto his knees behind me, and plunges his face between my thighs from behind.

My pants around my thighs and his tight hold on my arms keeps me locked in the same position. I can't get away, and as soon as he starts licking me, I don't want to get away.

He has to root his face hard between my thighs to burrow all the way into my swollen tissues. I'm so puffy and sensitive from last night that I start to orgasm right away.

I arch back and scream as his tongue lights me on fire, but he doesn't let me stand up. I push my slit back against his face and try to ride him to my completion.

He pulls back on my arms to cram me down on his face while he devours me to the ragged edge of madness. My screams spike out of control and I feel my juices gushing all over his face.

My sensitive skin picks up every detail of his hard lips and the scars on his face. He feels masterful and intoxicating like this.

Just when I think I can't take any more of this, he lets go of my arms, but he doesn't let me stand up. He grabs me with one arm over the top of my ass to hold me down and uses the other hand to lift my knee onto the counter.

He has to pull my pants down past my knees and then takes a massive bite of my juicy petals. I scream, but that's nothing compared to what happens when he drills his fingers into me at the same time.

I can't move except to thrash against the counter while he blasts me to the stars again and again.

This position makes me feel so raw and exposed and shameless. He's ravaging me exactly the way I want him to.

He turns me into a craven animal with nothing but the base desire for his body to fulfill my deepest need.

I don't know how long he plans to stay down there. He doesn't show any sign of slowing down.

He mauls me again and again in giant, devouring bites. He eats me out like a starving man at an all-you-can-eat buffet. He might stay there forever.

He doesn't stay there forever. He eventually stands up, pulls me off the counter, and stands me on my own feet.

I teeter in half-consciousness and moan from the last quivering waves of pleasure still coursing through me. My hand flies to my head. I can't think. I can barely see straight after what he just did to me.

Chapter 24: Sophie

C arter lifts me up, sits my bare ass on the cold, hard counter, and strips my pants the rest of the way off.

I can't fool myself about what he wants when he glares at me with such brutal passion. He pushes his hips between my thighs and pulls them apart to surround his waist.

He strips open his pants with one hand and drives into my saturated depths. My head starts to fall back in another torrential wave of ecstasy. I sob and then scream as he plunges in to the limit.

He grabs me by the back of the head and pulls me upright. "Look at me, baby," he rasps. "Look at me and see me."

My foggy eyes drift open to stare at his contorted face. His features go hard and mean as he bends over me.

His eyes leave me nowhere to run, but I can't focus on him for very long. He's already spiraling me into another dizzy climax.

He watches my eyes roll back in their sockets as he plows me to the first epic crescendo, but he doesn't finish there. Of course not. He'll keep going all night until we both pass out from exhaustion.

His hard eyes flicker from my trembling lips, my nostrils flaring with every tortured breath, to my eyes fighting to drag my gaze back into focus so I can see him.

I know how important it is to him that I look at him while we do it, but I can't focus my vision for more than a few seconds. I just hope he sees how much pleasure and rapture he gives me when he does this to me.

I feel his hands groping my breasts, pulling my shirt open, and tugging my bra down. My breasts fall out in front of him so he can see my whole body.

He doesn't kiss or suck them. He stays upright slamming into me harder and harder.

He makes my whole body quake and bounce from his rhythmic thrusts. My wetness spanks against his hips. I'm already so far gone that I only feel this endless river of bliss pouring into me through his shaft.

I get lost in the sea of sensation and mind-blowing cosmic explosions. I can't be sure how long he keeps going. It might be hours.

He gives no warning again when he straps both arms around my back, yanks me in tight, and slams home with a guttural snarl. He stays there while his shaft pulsates inside me and pumps me full of his seed.

That feeling spirals me out of my mind again. His seed.

I'm not on any birth control, but he doesn't ask nor does he seem to care. Is that where we're going with this?

I want to, but maybe he isn't ready for that. I have to tell him, but now isn't the right time. I can't think straight to say it right now anyway.

Thinking about his seed makes my head spin. His essence is so intoxicatingly powerful. I get another rush of orgasmic pleasure thinking about his seed taking me over and conquering my body from the inside.

He stays there locked with me, pants into my mouth, and growls in animal satisfaction until his energy dies.

I don't have a chance to move before he pulls away, scoops me up in his arms, and carries me to the living room.

He sits down on the couch, arranges me on his lap sitting sideways, and tucks my head against his neck.

I lie there whimpering with the last ebbs of delight twitching and shivering through my ragged body. His hot sauce gushes from my swollen, gaping channel and gets all over my ass.

I tremble in the throes of passion. I want him to do it to me again—and he will. He'll do it to me over and over as soon as he takes me back to his place. He'll never let me rest until he wrings every ounce of pleasure from my body.

He'll make me beg him for it even after he's already shattered my mind and senses with more pleasure than I can stand. I can never get enough of him.

Right now, though, I can only huddle here in the shelter of his arms and quiver as the tremors fade away to nothing.

He keeps stroking my hair and running his warm hands up my hips and legs. He kisses my hair and listens to me moaning, whining, sobbing, and whimpering from so much explosive pleasure.

Maybe now he'll realize how much I love him for giving me this. I can't let go of him. He's my only anchor in this storm.

I hide in his neck and shut my eyes, but my concerns from a few minutes ago come back to haunt me. I can't keep it to myself anymore.

"Dylan......" I cringe again and wince. "I'm so sorry."

"It's all right," he murmurs and kisses my hair again. "I know you see me for who I am."

I gulp hard. I want to tell him I love him, but I have to get this out first.

"I.....I'm not on any birth control," I blurt out.

He stiffens just for a second and then kisses me again. "That's all right with me if it's all right with you. I would love to go there with you if you feel comfortable with it. If you aren't...."

"I do! I just didn't know.....I thought.... You know...."

He pulls me deeper into his neck. "I want everything with you. I want us to go all the way—for the rest of our lives—if you want to."

I can't stand the emotion spilling out of me right now. For no reason I can think of, I burst into tears sobbing into his neck.

"I can't lose you, Dylan!" I wail. "I can't lose you ever again! Don't ever leave me again!"

He hugs me tighter. "I won't, baby. You'll never lose me again. We're going to be together from now on. We're going to have each other's backs exactly the way we promised we would. I'll never leave you. I swear it."

I cling to him while I sob. I don't know why I'm crying because I actually feel unbelievably happy. I've never felt so happy to have him with me. This is nothing to cry about.

All these orgasms—and everything else—they break down my last defenses. I can't hide anything from him. I need him too much.

My whole life has been a wreck without him. Now he's here. He holds me in his arms and protects me from my worst fears.

He doesn't even care that I'm crying after he gave me the greatest sexual pleasure of my life. He just keeps kissing, stroking, and holding me until I fall into limp exhaustion against his shoulder.

He doesn't move or try to get up. He could sit here forever. He really is content to just be with me no matter what we're doing.

I might have fallen asleep there because I wake up later. The light in the room looks different. The sun is lower. Night is coming on.

I stir and wrap my arms around Carter's neck tighter while I bring my brain back online.

He kisses my hair again. "Do you feel better now, baby?" he murmurs.

"I'm sorry," I mumble. "I must have dozed off."

"That's okay. You can fall asleep in my arms whenever you want."

I drag my eyes open. "We should probably....do something."

"We can stay here tonight if you want to."

Those words bring me back to reality real quick. I haul myself out of his arms and sit up.

I'm still wearing my bra and uniform shirt, but they're still pulled down under my breasts and push them up. I'm naked other than that.

I can't think clearly when I look around my apartment. I can't connect one thought to another well enough to decide on anything.

Carter rubs my back, rests his hand on my bare thigh, and then strokes my cheeks to push the hair out of my eyes. He stares deep into my soul from inches away.

"Stand up, put your clothes on, and get your stuff so I can take you to my place," he murmurs. "You aren't in any condition to do anything but go to bed."

I just want to wrap my arms around his neck, shut my eyes, and forget about everything, but he's right. Even if we stayed here tonight, I would have to stand up and walk into the bedroom.

I'm actually really hungry, too. I haven't eaten anything since lunchtime and neither has he. He's probably starving.

I drag myself off his lap and stand up. Once I start moving, my own momentum keeps me going.

I put my shirt and bra back on, pull on my pants, and lace up my work boots. Carter stands up, zips his pants, and tucks his shirt back into his waistband where it belongs.

Once we walk outside, no one will be able to see us as anything more than two paramedics going about our business.

I take a casserole pan of Sloppy-Joe pie out of the fridge along with a bag of salad mix and a bottle of salad dressing. I put everything on top of my duffel bag and meet Carter by the door.

He watches everything I do when I lock the apartment and head for the elevator. I have my hands full, but I would hold hands with him right now if I could.

I catch him eyeing me in the elevator, but he doesn't start anything. He minds his manners all the way out to the truck and contents himself with just kissing me when he settles me in the passenger seat.

We drive across town in silence. Neither of us says anything until we get upstairs to his apartment.

I felt like I was going to pass out when I first got off the couch. Now I feel energetic enough to make dinner for both of us.

I take the food to the kitchen, portion the casserole onto two plates, and microwave them while I set the table and make the salad.

Carter goes into the other room and then works on his phone at the kitchen counter while I work.

"What are you working on?" I ask.

"I'm just finalizing the Health and Safety audit for Howe Fire Department. I'll need to file it no matter the outcome of this complaint."

I make a face. "Andy is dumber than I thought if he doesn't withdraw the complaint now."

He smirks at me across the counter. "Chief Brewer really is a piece of work, isn't he? I almost had a heart attack when he said he would file a counter-complaint for harassment and disability discrimination."

"Well, Jesus! He's right, isn't he? Andy has had a burr under his saddle about you since day one. I don't see what reason he could possibly have to hate you so much if it doesn't have anything to do with the way you look."

Carter looks up at me and levels me with a direct stare. "It doesn't have anything to do with the way I look, baby. His attitude toward me has nothing to do with that."

"What is it, then? He's completely irrational when it comes to you. He had no reason to disobey a direct order from you in the middle of a critical scene."

"He hates me because of you!" he blurts out. "Don't tell me you don't see it."

I frown at him. "Me! What does this have to do with me? We never did anything that could make him hate you this much. All I did was talk to you at the barbecue. I talked to you the same way I would talk to anyone. The new Health and Safety officer could have been a woman—or an old man or an old lady. I would still have talked to them at the barbecue."

Now it's his turn to make a face. "Please, baby. You and I both know that was no normal conversation. You must have felt it or you wouldn't have told me about how bad things got for you in high school. There was a connection there even then. I didn't notice him watching us, but he must have been. He must have sensed that the conversation went way beyond what you would have with someone else."

I try to shrug that away. "You might be right."

"I am right. Why do you think you never told any of your crewmates about me?"

"I don't know. It never came up."

"So none of them ever asked you why you became a paramedic?"

"I didn't become a paramedic because of you. You had nothing to do with me becoming a paramedic. It had more to do with my brother dying."

"Think about it and you'll see I'm right," he tells me. "You've been working with these people for years. You were even in a relationship with Andy for I don't want to know how long and you never told any of them about me. That conversation we had at the barbecue was the very first conversation we ever had and you spilled your guts to me about what was the most painful, formative time of your life. You didn't just tell me you got depressed in high school and let your grades fall off and that's what stopped you from becoming a doctor. That would have been explanation enough, but you went much further than that. You told me all about losing your best friend and your brother's death and a whole lot more. We had a connection then—and you were attracted to me, weren't you? You were attracted to me even then. I know you were."

I turn bright red and try to smirk at him. "Can you blame me? You took your shirt off in front of all of us and went surfing. Every girl on that beach was lusting after you."

He bends over his phone. "I'm sure the married ones weren't—and I'm sure Oakleigh and Ainsley weren't, either."

I burst out laughing and put our dinner on the table. "Come over here and get something to eat."

He mutters under his breath, "Don't tempt me."

I blush again and pretend I don't know what he's talking about. We sit down at the table and start eating.

Chapter 25:
Carter

I study Sophie across the table while we eat the food she brought over from her apartment. The casserole is just as fantastic as the cake she brought to the barbecue. I might have to recruit her to cook for me all the time.

I can think of a lot of things I want to say to her right now, but words don't seem adequate to express them all.

I slide my hand across the table and she takes it. She beams at me and we hold hands while we eat.

"You okay?" she asks.

I nod at nothing. I'm more than okay. "This casserole is great. Thank you for doing this. I was just trying to decide what to make for you."

She bursts out in nervous laughter. Her eyelashes dip when she looks down at her plate. "I like to be organized. It saves time and effort when I come home tired after a shift."

"Smart. So.....how would you feel about moving in with a guy you've only been seeing for two days?"

She turns bright red and barely looks at me. "I would love to."

I squeeze her hand. "Would you rather live here or at your apartment? Yours seems nicer."

She won't look at me at all now and she doesn't eat. She pushes her food back and forth and mumbles into her dish. "I like it here better. You're here."

I find myself laughing. "I would be there, too, baby. That's the whole point."

She finally raises her eyes to me. They blaze with some mysterious light. Her voice trembles when she asks, "Dylan?"

"Yes?" I ask.

She takes a long time to work up the courage to say what's on her mind. "Do you remember....what you said earlier.....about me not being on birth control?"

My heart skips a beat. "Yeah? What about it?"

"If we.....if we're really gonna do this....."

I stop her by squeezing her hand again. "You said you wanted to do it."

"I do!" she exclaims. "I want that more than anything."

I can't stand having this table between us and she isn't eating anyway. I stand up, walk around to her side of the table, lift her hand to draw her to her feet, and take her back to my chair where I sit her sideways on my lap.

God damn, she feels good here! I want to eat dinner like this every night.

I pet her hair and arms and kiss her right behind her ear. "Now tell me what's on your mind."

"I was just thinking....." She has a hard time looking at me. "I was just thinking....if we're really going to do this—like go all the way like you said—we should probably buy a house."

I raise my eyebrows. "Really? Do you want to?"

"I mean.....if we keep having unprotected sex.....we're going to need one."

I blink at her when I realize what she's saying. What else could us having unprotected sex mean?

I should have thought of that before I went and shot her full of my load these last two days, but it's a little late to worry about that now.

I didn't think of it. I should have, but I was just too damn over the moon about doing it with her. I didn't think it through.

Thinking about it now makes me rock hard in seconds. Every time I do it with her, every time I do unload into her, I'm taking the chance that I could get her pregnant.

I could have done it last night. I could have done it on her kitchen counter just a little while ago.

Thinking that makes me so damn hot for her. I can barely stop myself from tearing her clothes off right here on the dining room table.

I want to pump her full of my seed and make her grow big and round and ripe and full of my baby—all of them.

Holy shit! This is really happening. She says she wants that. She says she wants to go all the way with me—even as far as buying a house together.

She's absolutely right. We would need a house if we had kids together. Why not now? Why wait?

She looks up and her voice trembles even more when she stares at me. "Are you okay? Say something. You're scaring me."

I don't seem to be able to drag my awareness back to reality. I keep seeing her stomach swollen and heavy, her breasts bulging with milk, a tiny baby sucking on her nipples, and a houseful of kids running around both of us.

I almost bust my nut right here just thinking about it. This adrenaline pumping through my veins feels like exploding in the biggest climax of my life. God, I want that!

I want to see her groaning with the weight of my baby inside her. I want to see her screaming in childbirth. I want to see her breastfeeding my children.

I want to walk into the house after an exhausting day and hear the kids screaming and see the house a wreck from their play. Jesus Christ, I want that so bad!

My cock strains to get inside her so I can plant the seed to make it happen right now. I want to do it with her and never stop doing it until I get her so knocked up she can't see straight.

I want to see my jiz gurgling out of her swollen gash so I know I gave her enough to fill her to overflowing.

Her eyes hypnotize me when I finally meet her gaze. "I want that, baby," I croak. "I want it all—always and forever. You're right. We should buy a house. Do you own your apartment? I'm only renting this one—but I have savings—enough for a down payment."

She brightens up and then her features blanch with a sudden wave of terror. "I have savings, too—and I own the apartment."

I cock my head to study her. "What's wrong? Is this what you want?"

Her face spasms. "I'm just...scared....you know?"

I pull her down on my shoulder. "Me, too, baby, but we're going to get through it together. We both want this. It's going to be good." I bend across the table and pull her plate to my side. "Eat your dinner and let's go to bed. We have a lot to do and we both have to work tomorrow."

I keep her on my lap while we both eat in silence. She doesn't interrupt my thoughts—my daydreams and fantasies about the life I'm going to have with her.

I fantasized about a lot of things when I was in high school. I even fantasized about bending her over the kitchen counter, devouring her from behind, and then drilling her until we both exploded in ecstasy.

I never once dreamed I would be talking about buying a house and having kids with her. I don't know if I can handle the emotion and excitement boiling out of me when I think about that.

This is the final frontier. It's completely uncharted territory.

I can't stop touching her, but I keep it light during the meal. I stroke up and down her back, massage her neck and shoulders, and comb her hair out of her face while she eats.

Her body pulsates with so much potential right here on my lap. Her body is the fertile ground from which this whole fantasy will grow and become real.

I just have to activate her. I have to press the right buttons to give her so much pleasure she won't be able to resist. I have to master her body and conquer it so it bears the fruit we want it to bear.

The thought of impregnating her drives me out of my mind. I have to restrain myself not to take her again right now.

The same thought forces me to sit still and wait. I have to be extra gentle with her. I can treat her like an animal in the bedroom, but I also have to take care of her.

I have to make absolutely certain that she's protected and that she feels comfortable, safe, and enthusiastic at all times.

It's my job to make sure she feels comfortable enough to tell me what she wants, how she wants it, and if anything is bothering her.

We don't have to jump right into buying a house this minute. We've been seeing each other for less than a week.

I have to slow myself down. I have to dig in for the long haul. We'll have plenty of time for all of that.

She zones out while she eats. She brings her fork to her mouth on autopilot. She doesn't engage and her expression goes blank. The mind-numbing fatigue of the last two days is creeping back in if it hasn't taken over already.

I wait until she finishes before I stand her up, pick up her bag from the floor next to the front door, and take her into the bedroom. "Change out of your uniform and get into bed, baby," I tell her. "I'll clean up the table."

I leave her there, stack the dishes in the dishwasher, and put the leftover food in the fridge. I lock up the house, turn off the lights, and go into the bedroom just as she's coming out of the bathroom with her hair hanging loose.

My package throbs again when I see her wearing a white wife-beater tank top with no bra and baggy pajama pants. Oh, my God! I can't stand how hot she looks.

I pull down the covers for her so she can get into bed. She snuggles into the pillow—my pillow. This is my bed. She's getting into my bed.

Her eyes keep drifting halfway shut while she watches me put my stuff away, kick off my boots, and change my clothes.

I become aware of her eyes tracking my every move when I take my shirt off and change into my pajama pants. Her eyes trace every ripple of my scars, front and back.

No one has ever studied my scars as closely as she does. Everyone else I've ever met always avoids looking at my scars whenever possible. Even my own family members try to pretend they're avoiding looking at them even when they can't stop staring.

Her gaze makes me self-conscious. I'm not totally comfortable with the awe and admiration in those eyes. I've always considered myself ugly, but she doesn't look at me like I am.

She rolls onto her back and stretches her soft arms to me when I get into bed. She kisses me and presses her magnificent body against me.

I scoot down under the covers, wrap my arms around her waist, and bury my face in the softness of her breasts right under her shirt. This is going to be my new favorite place to sleep.

She sighs and hugs my head against her. Her body floods my mind with so many pictures of our future together.

I just can't stop my mouth from nibbling sideways to her nipples. They poke through her shirt and tempt me to mouth them until she moans. Her thighs slide against mine.

I should let her sleep. I need sleep, too, after our marathon last night, but this aching throb between my legs won't leave me alone.

My body takes over. I have to get inside her to unload on her—just once. I have to start the growth process right now.

I grab for her ass, miss my aim, and wind up sliding my fingers between her thighs from behind.

She mews in excruciating desire and her fingers dig into my scalp when she crushes my head deeper into her breasts.

I inhale them through her shirt, pull her pajama pants aside just enough, and plow into her moist, hot, succulent channel.

I only have to think about getting her pregnant to get throbbing hard instantly. I stroke slowly so I don't blast off too quickly.

She moans in my ears and presses her sweet lips to my scalp while she rises to the skies. Her beautiful, plaintive screams carry me into such a delicious fantasy.

I pull her thighs around me while we're both still lying on our sides. She doesn't struggle. She melts into my arms and moves with my rhythm.

I can't hold out for long, though—not when she tastes and smells and feels so good. Her engorged channel swallows me in pillowy wet softness. It's the perfect place for my seed to take root.

I pull back from her chest and look straight into her eyes drunken with sex. She knows what I'm doing because I'm not using any protection.

Can she feel it through my shaft? Can she feel all the potential flooding her from me?

Her lips shiver with the strain and her eyes roll back as she screams again and again. I can't tear my eyes away from her angelic face as I thrust deep inside her and eject my load into her deepest, darkest recesses.

Even after I finish and she lies whimpering and sobbing in my arms, I can't pull out of her. I want to feel her muscles rippling down my shaft just begging for more. I'm gonna give her so much more. I'm never going to stop—not ever.

This woman is the foundation of my future. She's my joy and my sustenance. She's the fulfillment of so many dreams I never even knew I had.

I leave my slab inside her and she moans again when I bury my face in her chest. She trembles, but I don't start up again. I let her drift off....and I drift off into all the dreams swimming around in my head.

Chapter 26: Carter

I kiss Sophie on the forehead and leave the bedroom while she's still asleep. She doesn't have to show up for work until a later shift. I want her to sleep as long as possible. She needs it.

I pause in the doorway to look back at her. She lies in my bed with her glowing golden head on my pillow and my sheets and blankets lying over her immaculate body.

I never thought this would really happen, but it is. She's mine. She's living in my house and sleeping in my bed. She wants to stay here with me always.

Just looking at her like this feels like a distant dream. She's so beautiful that she doesn't seem real.

All the trouble I've been going through these last ten years—none of it seems real anymore.

I have to remind myself that I'm still a scarred monster that kids scream and run from when they see me in public.

I have a hard time remembering any of that when I think about how much my life has changed.

No one at Howe Firehouse treats me like that—apart from Andy. The rest of the crew treats me as if I look the same as they do. None of them seems to notice it anymore.

I tear myself away with a wrench, shut the bedroom door, and slip out of the apartment.

Driving to the firehouse is another surreal experience. I'm working here now and I'll stay here. I don't want to leave and I don't have to. I have no reason to.

Being a Health and Safety officer traveling from one firehouse to another worked out well for me because I never stayed in one place for long.

None of those crews wanted me to stay in one place for long. They all held me at a distance and I held them at a distance. I did my audit and left without making any connections with anyone.

Things are so different here at Howe. The crew had the usual reaction when I first walked into the room that first day.

I can't think of a single time when any of them has even mentioned the way I look—apart from Andy, of course—oh, and the time I went surfing at the barbecue. My appearance is just a fact of life around here now.

They were all thrilled when I said I was going to stay. None of them questioned it. They congratulated me—but they also congratulated each other. They want me.

I get an overwhelming feeling of almost painful happiness when I park my truck and get out to go into the firehouse. I can't wait to see all of them—the firehouse family.

They all use those words—and they actually mean it. They treat each other like family and they really mean it when they say I'm part of that.

I walk into the garage and immediately field a whole bunch of greetings from the crew. Keith, Billy, Danny, Vince, Theo, Josh, Chris, Brooke, and Naomi stand around the bulletin board having a heated discussion about the roster.

"Hey man!" Josh calls over to me. "It looks like John is rostering you on the rescue truck for all your shifts. You could swap out onto the ambulances if you want to."

"I'm good on the truck," I call back from the locker room. "Unless you think I can't handle it or something."

"*We* usually work on the trucks," Chris tells me. "It's unusual for John to roster a new paramedic on the trucks right off the bat."

"It's obvious why, though, isn't it?" Keith interjects. "Carter is a firefighter, too. We're already shorthanded. Why waste him?"

"That's my point, see?" Chris goes on. "We already have two paramedics on the truck. We don't need three of them."

"Danny isn't a paramedic," I point out. "He's injured, so technically, I'm filling in for him."

"But we're short on paramedics to man the ambulances," Brooke adds. "Drew and George are together on Unit 1. You should be there."

"Then John would have to bump one of them off the shift and we would be short a firefighter on the truck," Billy tells her. "Just pretend Carter isn't a paramedic for a change."

"By that logic, George should be on the truck and Carter should be on the ambulance with Drew," Naomi chimes in. "Then we would have both ambulances crewed by paramedics and the same number of firefighters rostered on the truck."

"But George doesn't have the same firefighter qualifications that Carter has," Josh points out. "George isn't certified to work on the truck at all. He and Drew can only work on the ambulances."

I raise both hands. "You kids should probably talk to Chief Brewer about this—not me. I don't make the rules."

"Weren't you working with him on the roster before all this other shit happened?" Keith asked.

"I was, and from what I saw, the greatest minds of scientific code-cracking couldn't wrangle that roster into anything remotely resembling something that would pass a Health and Safety audit. If he put me on the truck, that's where I'm working. If we get a call with a whole ton of critical patients, I'll be working on them either way no matter which vehicle I ride in to get to the scene."

Keith rubs his chin. "I suppose I can't argue with that."

"Are we checking the vehicles or are we standing around doing the Chief's job for him?" I pull open the truck door and climb in.

Brooke and Josh get into the back and start checking the paramedic's drug box.

I don't get involved. I pay attention to checking the firefighting equipment—like it somehow makes a difference which job I do.

All of that is going to go out the window as soon as we get a call. The firefighters will fight fires. The paramedics will treat patients. The EMTs will help the paramedics and drive the ambulances. The roster doesn't mean that much.

The rest of the crew all breaks up to do their own start-of-shift checks, too.

A few minutes later, Andy waltzes through the garage doors. He's rostered on the other ambulance with Emily Montgomery as his EMT.

I pretend not to see him and he pretends not to see me. He meets up with Emily and I don't see either of them again while they check their unit and their equipment.

Chief Brewer shows up in a little while and has to explain to everyone all over again that there is no way on God's green Earth to get the roster into any kind of order that fills all the shifts and makes everybody happy at the same time.

We all just have to deal with it—which is just fine with me.

We finish our checks and everyone retires to the breakroom. Billy, Vince, Theo, and Jacob are all working on their latest professional development booklets.

The rest of us paramedics sit around laughing at them and trying to explain things to them when they don't understand.

"How the hell are we supposed to understand how glucagon causes glycogen release from the pancreas?" Billy snarls. "Why can't they just use normal English to explain these things?"

Brooke bends over and hugs him before she goes back to cleaning out the breakroom fridge. "You'll figure it out. I know you will."

"So glycogen releases sugar from the muscles?" Jacob asks.

"No, glycogen IS the sugar that gets released from the muscles," Josh explains. "Glycogen is a sugar-storage molecule. It stores sugars from your food in your muscles and in your pancreas. Glucagon causes the pancreas and the muscles to release their glycogen stores so more sugar is available to the muscles during flight-or-fight situations."

"Wait a minute! That can't be right," Vince counters. "This says glucagon is released from the pancreas—not glycogen."

Chris laughs. "Both are released by the pancreas, sweetie. The pancreas releases glucagon in order to release its own glycogen stores."

"That's stupid!" Billy snaps. "Why does it have to release glucagon in the first place? Why can't it skip a step, release the damn glycogen, and call it good?"

I laugh along with the others, but I don't say anything. These guys have a hard enough time understanding this stuff already.

"The good news is that we can inject glucagon into diabetic patients to release their glycogen stores," Josh explains.

Billy frowns. "What good will that do? Aren't diabetics high in sugar already?"

"Sometimes they can take their insulin and then forget to eat—or they don't eat enough. They get dangerously low on blood sugar—which is much more dangerous than having high blood sugar. Glucagon corrects this—at least temporarily. It stops diabetic shock until the person can correct the imbalance on their own."

Billy runs his fingers through his hair and sighs. "I don't see why a grunt firefighter needs to understand this."

"You'll need to understand it if you ever get EMT certified," George chimes in, and right then, we get a call.

The alarm blasts through the firehouse and we all drop what we're doing to rush downstairs.

I load up in the truck with Keith, Billy, Theo, Vince, Josh, and Brooke. "House on fire—West Springfield Road!" Billy yells over the siren. "Fifteen patients with smoke inhalation already outside! Another ten unaccounted for still in the building!"

Keith spins around to stare at him. "Twenty-five patients! Crap!"

No one says anything after that. We don't wise-crack on the way to the scene. The other firefighters and I concentrate on checking and rechecking our equipment.

Billy brings up a floor plan of the house and the four of us firefighters go over it on our way out of town.

Josh and Brooke murmur low to each other while they organize the supplies in their drug box and load up extra gear into their jump kit. They swap out some of the medical items for burn kits, bandages, and burn blankets.

Josh also gets out the triage tags and hands them up to Theo. "You better take these. You, Drew, George, and Emily will need to triage the patients who are already out of the house while we extricate anyone from inside. You could transport anyone who's critical before we get the rest of the victims out."

Theo nods. "Sure thing. Just send the order over to Andy so he understands why we're taking Emily."

Josh explains the situation to Billy who radios the new order to Andy and the three EMTs. Chief Brewer chimes in on the conversation to back up the decision.

Andy acknowledges it as professionally as anyone could ask him to. If he gets his panties in a twist about Josh assigning Emily to triage, Andy doesn't give it away.

He would have to be bone stupid to argue with Chief Brewer about something like that.

The house in question is an isolated farmhouse way out in the countryside. It's the only building for miles around except for a large wooden barn five hundred yards away on the same property.

We find out the minute we roll into the driveway why there were so many people on the premises.

A giant white flower arch covers the driveway entrance. White satin sashes, white balloons, and white streamers hang from the shrubs lining the driveway.

A white flower arch stands in the front yard with a red-carpet aisle passing between dozens of chairs set up in rows.

A long row of buffet tables circles one half of the yard. Champagne fountains, towers of cut fruit, and an enormous white wedding cake weigh down the tables with every kind of treat a bridal party could ask for.

Dozens of people wearing tuxes and bridesmaids' dresses stand around outside. Some sit on the grass and some lie down. The bride sits slumped on the grass with soot all over her dress, hair, veil, and face.

Everyone crowds to the other side of the yard and watches in horror as fire destroys the house on what is supposed to be a happy occasion.

Chapter 27: Carter

The crew immediately faces a problem trying to get the trucks and ambulances close enough to the burning house.

A bunch of caterers' vans block the driveway. We have to go through a nightmare ordeal of getting the caterers to move.

Chief Brewer shows up and storms through the crowd barking orders at everyone. The bride's father, whom I assume owns this house, races over to us and intercepts Chief Brewer.

"The caterers were all in the kitchen!" the bride's father explains. "That's where the fire started. We heard an explosion—and none of the caterers came out. They're all still in there—and they all have the keys to these vans."

Chief Brewer's features go hard. No sane person would want to stand in his way when he looks like that.

He turns around and points at all of us. The fire trucks are still too far out in the driveway.

"All of you get into the house on the double and get those people out!" he barks. "EMTs—start triaging these patients and transport anyone who's critical. Keith—you supervise getting those hoses rigged up." He turns back to the bride's father. "We're going to need you to set us up with the biggest water source you have. These trucks don't have enough to suppress the fire and we're too far away."

"No problem. I can hook you up the farm supply," the bride's father replies. "It has a flow rate of five hundred gallons per minute. Is that enough?"

"It will have to be." Chief Brewer yells at all of us. "Let's get moving, people!"

We all pile in. I pull on my SCBA, start the airflow to my mask, and fit it over my face under my helmet.

I wait just long enough to hear the bride's father give us an explanation of where the caterers are—or where they were.

We have to go around to the back door and break through a burning wall to get inside. Billy, Cameron Santiago from the ladder truck, Vince, and Theo back up Josh, Andy, and me to go in and look for the missing people.

The guys hack through the wall with their axes. The flames have already eaten through the boards so we get inside easily.

We break through into the hall between the kitchen and the dining room. Flames cover the ceiling. They're already starting to climb down the walls, but the floor and side walls are still intact almost to the height of my head.

We go into the kitchen. Fire consumes one whole half of the room—the side where the stove and ovens used to be.

A wall of flame blocks us from going over there, but we don't have to. If anyone is over there, they're long dead.

We can circle the big worktable. The caterers set up warning trays here before carrying them to the buffet tables outside. The trays are all empty. The caterers must not have started filling them yet.

We don't find anyone in here. I move my head close to Josh so he can hear me through my mask.

"That side of the kitchen isn't big enough for all the missing people!" I holler. "They must have been somewhere else when the explosion went off!"

"We have some time!" he yells back. "Let's check the rest of the downstairs before the whole house gets involved!"

He heads back down the hallway toward the dining room. The rest of the ground floor occupies the area in front of that. The kitchen and dining room are the last rooms in the very back of the house.

The firefighters go in front of us throwing open every door they come to. One leads to a bathroom—also empty. Another opens into a broom closet. There's no one in there.

Josh goes in front of me with Andy bringing up the rear. I search every inch of the place and don't see any people.

The firefighters yell out when they get near the dining room. I see over their shoulders that the missing caterers are sheltering in the dining room—the place farthest away from the flames.

The firefighters rush them. Josh and I charge forward to join them, but right at that moment, a catastrophic explosion goes off behind my back.

The shockwave makes me stagger, and at the same moment, the two air supply hoses leading to my mask blow off. The valves rupture and smoke and burning gas pour into my mask.

They burn my throat and lungs and choke me. I fight to breathe and claw at the mask to get it off in time.

At the same moment, the regulator on my oxygen tank fails. It explodes off the tank and starts venting compressed oxygen so fast and hard that the force drives me down on my knees.

Josh and the firefighters don't notice anything wrong with me. They're too busy surrounding the caterers and taking care of the injured.

I flounder trying to get the mask off before I suffocate. I can't move my arms with the oxygen tank strapped to my back.

I wind up throwing off my helmet, yanking off my mask, and then I fall over under the weight of my tank before I throw off the shoulder straps, too.

I'm just trying to sit up without getting every ounce of my flesh scorched off my bones—again.

That's when I notice Andy lying face down on the floor a few feet away. He's out cold and doesn't move to save himself from the flames licking and woofing all around him.

Monstrous flames plume out of the kitchen behind us. Only his position lying flat on the floor saves him from certain death.

All restraint flies out the window. I've been through this before. No way in hell am I going through that again—and I won't let anyone else go through it, either.

I dive for him, grab him by his turnouts, and heave. His SCBA makes him weigh a ton, but I can't risk him suffering from smoke inhalation, too.

I take a split second to check his apparatus to make sure it's still working. It is. He can still breathe clean air.

I can't, but that doesn't matter. I take two fistfuls of his turnouts and drag him another ten feet down the hall before I collapse. I don't dare to stand up or even get onto my knees.

The flames keep crawling lower down the walls. The second explosion from the kitchen blocks any path to the hole we used to come in here.

I have one chance of escape. I have to get Andy to the dining room.

I just hope and pray one of the guys notices us gone and comes back for us. Andy and I are both finished if they don't notice.

I put all my faith in Josh. As soon as he starts taking care of the patients, he'll realize he's the only paramedic left. He'll send someone to look for us. I just hope Andy and I are still alive when that happens.

All the bad blood and hostility between me and Andy goes right out the window. He's a fellow firefighter and he's in trouble. I have to get him out no matter what.

Smoke and hot air blister my lungs. I have no choice but to gasp in big mouthfuls of all that scorching air just to keep going.

I pull him another fifteen feet. Every pull costs me every scrap of my strength. I won't be able to keep this up for much longer.

I steal a glance over my shoulder toward the dining room. I don't see anyone in it anymore. I pray to God Almighty the guys found another way out of the house.

At least the flames haven't gotten into the dining room yet.

I take hold of Andy's jacket to pull him the last ten feet across the threshold. I'm clear of the flames. I can stand up here.

I push myself to my feet and swivel around Andy's body to pick him up in an over-the-shoulder fireman's carry. I'll be able to look for another way out much easier that way.

I stand over him, but at that moment, another bone-crushing explosion goes off in the kitchen behind me.

This one obliterates most of that side of the house and a wave of burning timbers, volcanic coals, and billowing flame plasters me across the back.

I barely have time to dive on top of Andy before all that crap smashes into me from behind. Then it buries me and Andy under a mountain of scorching debris.

I bury my head under my arms, but I can't stay here. Devouring heat burns me through my turnouts. I have to get out of here.

I strike out to throw off burning boards, twisted pipes, smoldering embers, and a whole lot of broken, shattered remains of stuff I can't identify.

I shake myself to get the stuff off me and yell in pain when I feel bruises and broken bones all over me.

Actually, that isn't right. Only my left arm is broken, but the rest of me is battered to hell and I howl in agony every time I move. I have to get out of here. This is my last chance or I'll die in here.

I grab Andy a second time. I can't lift him and now the flames are eating their way into the dining room. I don't even know if I can get out that way, but I sure as hell can't escape any other way.

The dining room is the best-protected spot in the whole house. If I can't find anywhere, I'll have no choice but to return to the same spot where the crew found the caterers.

I'll have to use Andy's SCBA and pass it back and forth between both of us so we can both breathe for as long as possible. Then I'll just have to hope and pray someone finds us in time. I can't get out of here on my own.

I haul Andy into the dining room. I break down roaring and even sobbing in pain each time I put pressure on my crushed body, but I have to keep going.

I drag him around the dining room table to where I last saw the trapped caterers.

I get Andy all the way over there before I see that the guys have hacked another hole in the outer house wall. The breach opens into the backyard.

I really do break down in tears of relief when I see it. I just have to get myself and Andy out of this house. Then I can collapse and never stand up again.

I pull Andy all the way over to the breach before another bone-shattering explosion goes off somewhere in the house. I don't see where it comes from.

It doesn't make the fire worse—not on this side of the house. The concussion rocks the floor and I slam down onto my side closer to the hole. I drag my sorry ass over there gasping for one breath of cool air in this inferno.

I fall there wheezing and whimpering before I manage to sit up and grab Andy again. I pull him one last yard toward the breach.

I have to lie there to gather my strength for the last final push. More impacts keep striking the house again and again where I can't see them.

I have to sit up. I have to finish this, but before I can move, someone dives through the hole behind me, grabs me by the turnouts, and yanks me through the opening.

I slam down on the ground and Josh, Brooke, Billy, and Keith all surround me talking at once.

"Andy...." I croak. "Get Andy....."

"We got him, man!" Keith tells me. "Lie still. We got him. You're safe! You're out! You both are!"

Brooke covers my face with an oxygen mask, but I can't stay conscious a second longer. My eyes drift shut and I black out.

Chapter 28:
Sophie

I have to control my pulse when I walk into the firehouse for my shift. I woke up alone in Carter's apartment—in his bed.

We're going to live together. We're going to buy a house and start a family together.

I have to stop myself from getting little rushes of thrilling excitement. This is happening. I can't believe it. All my dreams are coming true.

I don't know how I'll be able to stop smirking like an idiot the minute I see him.

As soon as I walk in, I see that both trucks and both ambulances are gone. The crew must be out on a call.

The second shift stands around talking in an undertone on one side of the empty garage.

"Hi, guys!" I tell them when I walk in.

They don't greet me the way they usually do. They give me strange looks and their conversation falls silent.

I really hope I didn't do something to offend my co-workers. I'll have to find out what it is and make it right—but I can't remember doing anything.

I walk past them to put my backpack in my locker. I'm just getting ready to close it when John walks in. "I need you to come up to my office, Sophie," he tells me. "I need to talk to you."

My throat goes dry. "Is something wrong? Am I in trouble for something? I don't know what it is."

"You aren't in trouble," he murmurs. "Please....come upstairs. We need to talk."

I gulp. Going up to John's office is never a good time.

I have no choice but to follow him. At least maybe I'll find out why everyone is looking at me funny downstairs.

John waits for me to enter and shuts the door behind me. "Sit down—please," he tells me in an undertone. This must be serious.

I sit down and perch on the edge of the seat with my hands clamped between my knees.

He sits in his chair behind his desk, takes a deep breath, and launches in. "Carter got hurt on the job earlier. He's in the hospital.....and he's critical...."

My jaw drops in silent horror. I can't even make a sound. Dylan....he can't be hurt....

"He went into a burning house to get some trapped people out," John goes on in his funeral voice. "There was an explosion and Andy got hit. He got knocked out and Carter went back for him. The rest of the crew was too busy rescuing the victims to see what was happening until it was too late. Carter dragged Andy to safety, but another explosion went off and Carter got hit by a bunch of burning debris. He got injured, but he still managed to pull Andy to safety before the crew found them."

I have to gulp before I can get my voice working. "Are you saying....Carter....is injured and critical in the hospital....from saving Andy?!"

"Yeah," John breathes. "He saved Andy's life.....and that's not all. The guys put the fire out and I went over there to start the arson survey."

I gasp out loud. "Are you saying the fire was arson?!"

"No, it wasn't. It was operator error by some wedding caterers—but that's not what I'm telling you. Carter wasn't wearing his SCBA when the guys pulled him out. That was the problem. He suffered severe smoke inhalation and respiratory burns because he wasn't wearing his apparatus."

"That's ridiculous!" I practically shriek. "Carter is way too practical to take off his SCBA in the middle of a full-blown fire! No way!"

"That's what Keith said—and Josh, Vince, and all the others who were with him said the same thing—but it was obvious at the scene that he hadn't been wearing his SCBA through almost the entire call. When they told me, I went over there to investigate and I found what was left of his mask and oxygen tank in the wreckage."

"And?!" I demand. "What did you find? You wouldn't be telling me this if there wasn't some kind of foul play involved."

He heaves an almighty sigh. "Someone tampered with his SCBA. The supply hoses to the mask failed in the middle of the call and the regulator blew off the tank. It knocked him down and then he had to take off the mask so he wouldn't suffocate. That's what caused the smoke inhalation and respiratory burns."

"Are you saying....who the hell would sabotage his SCBA?! This is....." I stop with the words on my lips.

"It's attempted murder." John turns his computer monitor around so I can see the screen. He hits a button on his keyboard.

The screen wakes up and starts playing security camera footage from the firehouse garage. The timestamp says, *3 AM,* last night.

The footage shows Andy climbing into the rescue truck, pulling one of the SCBAs from inside, setting the tank on the floor, and tinkering with the mask and the regulator valve.

I can't believe what I'm seeing. Andy.....he actually tried to kill Carter. This is unbelievable.

We all knew Andy was a jerk. I never thought he was dangerous.

This is beyond anything I've ever seen anywhere in this job—and it's one of our own crew.

One of our crew actually tried to kill another member of our crew. This is beyond terrible.

"Andy is downtown getting questioned by the Police," John murmurs when he switches off the footage. "They're confronting him with the evidence. We'll hear as soon as he either admits guilt or calls a lawyer." He stands up. "Come on. I'll drive you to the hospital."

I sit and stare at the blank computer screen. I can't move. This isn't happening.

John doesn't wait for me to respond. He walks around the desk, takes hold of my elbow, and leads me out of the firehouse.

No one talks to either of us on our way outside. He puts me in the passenger seat of his support pickup and drives me across town in silence.

My dream come true can't end like this. Carter has to be okay. I can't lose him—not now.

I barely see anything outside the windows before John parks in the hospital parking lot. He leads me inside. We ride the elevator up to the ICU.

We stop outside a room with a burn victim lying on the bed. He has a tube going into his nose and an ET tube down his throat. A ventilator inflates his lungs every few seconds and the ECG next to his bed bleeps every time it records his heartbeat.

One of his arms lies across his chest with a splint, a sling, and thick bandages around it.

John leaves me standing there staring at this thing in the bed. Carter looks absolutely awful. He doesn't look at all like the strong, vibrant man I've been falling in love with these past few days.

None of the vitality enlivens his face or his eyes. He looks half dead with all those burns all over his face, head, neck, and arms.

John talks to the nurses at the nurses' station and then to the doctors who happen to be going through the ward just then.

I have to struggle to pay attention when three doctors come over to tell me how Carter is.

"Could you tell Sophie what you just told me?" John asks.

The doctors all give me a sympathetic look. "The good news is that he didn't sustain any additional burns—nothing serious at least," an older doctor with grey hair tells me. "He has a broken arm and he suffered very superficial first-degree burns to his back, but that's all. The rest of his injuries are mostly just severe bruising and soft-tissue injury to his back, spine, and shoulders."

"The smoke inhalation and respiratory burns are his most critical injuries," a middle-aged woman doctor tells me. "The paramedics intubated him in the field because he couldn't protect his airway, but we expect him to make a full recovery from that. We'll keep him sedated for another twenty-four hours until we're sure we can extubate him safely."

I swallow hard. I should thank these people for reassuring me that Carter is going to be okay, but I can't make a sound.

I turn back to the room in a stunned daze. I hardly recognize him like this.

John waits what seems like a long time before he puts his arm around my shoulder and squeezes. "I'm going to go back to the firehouse to check on the rest of the crew. You have my number if you need anything. Call me if his condition changes."

I barely notice when he kisses the side of my head and leaves. I can't stop staring at Carter.

The rational part of my brain understands what the doctors said. Carter will recover from this. His arm will heal and he'll get his strength back.

The rest of me gets trapped in this suspended trance where nothing exists but right now.

Carter is lying in this hospital bed because he saved Andy's life. Carter is a true professional. He would never let some petty dispute between him and Andy interfere with doing his job.

Andy is downtown getting questioned by the Police—which means Andy isn't in the hospital—not even for minor injuries. He got out of the house without a scratch while Carter is in ICU with tubes going into every part of his body.

He has to be okay. He just has to. I can't face the future without him—not after everything we've been through.

He's too tough to let something like this get him down. I know that. His first fire was way worse than this.

He won't take a year and a half to recover from this. His broken arm will take the longest to heal.

Andy actually tried to kill Carter. The smoke inhalation and respiratory burns are the worst of his injuries. He wouldn't have any of that if he had been wearing his SCBA during the call.

Attempted murder. I have trouble even thinking those words. They don't seem to fit with someone who is a certified firefighter and paramedic.

Someone like that couldn't actually try to kill someone. A firefighter and paramedic in good standing couldn't actually try to kill another firefighter and paramedic. That just isn't possible.

And yet it is. I saw the video footage myself. I wouldn't have believed it otherwise, but now I have to.

I take a few steps into the room, but I still can't bring myself to go near Carter when he's like this.

I should hold his hand. I should talk to him, but I can't do that. I can't think.

I stagger away down the hall to a waiting room at the end of the ICU. I sink into a chair and stare at the wall.

Dylan and I were so happy last night. I've never been happier than when I fell asleep in his arms.

He must have been just as happy when he woke up this morning and left for work while I was still asleep in his bed.

I don't want to be anywhere else. I want to be there in his bed when he comes home late at night. I want to be there for him to put his arms around me when he falls asleep at night.

Will I have to lie awake fearing the worst until I hear his truck pull into the driveway? I hear the other firehouse wives talk about their fears.

All of those concerns seemed so far away from me until now. Now I'm one of those women—hanging around a hospital waiting room waiting for the axe to fall and for someone to come tell me what the rest of my life is going to be like.

I cringe when I think about John losing his first wife. What a nightmare he must have been living all those years.

I can't imagine losing your life partner like that. One of them getting injured is torture enough.

They've all been through it, too. Keith got shot in the head by a raving madman. Billy got run over by another murderous psycho's car.

Now it's my turn to sit here with the weight of my whole future hanging in the balance.

The doctor could walk through that door any second now and drop a bomb on me that would destroy my life.

Losing Dylan now would be so much worse than losing him the first time. I couldn't survive losing him like this.

I'm still sitting there in a fog when Brooke, Chris, Josh, Billy, Vince, Theo, and Keith roll up.

They surround me all talking at once. "How is he, Sophie?" Chris asks.

"Um...." I drag my senses back to awareness. "He's....he's gonna be okay. The doctors say his smoke inhalation isn't too bad. They plan to extubate him tomorrow....and after that, they expect him to make a full recovery."

Brooke passes her hand across her eyes. "Phew! I was so worried when we got him out of the building and he couldn't breathe. We thought he was a goner for sure."

I blink at her. *"You* got him out of the building—all of you?"

"He got himself out of the building," Josh corrects. "We never would have gotten him or Andy if Carter hadn't pulled them both so close to the exit."

"We were all on the crew with him," Vince tells me. "He was right behind us. We didn't see him go back for Andy until after we got the other patients out."

"I don't care what anyone says," Keith growls. "He did NOT take off his SCBA in the middle of that call. Something must have happened."

"You mean...you guys don't know?!" I exclaim. "John didn't tell you?!"

"Tell us what?" Chris asks.

"Andy...." I have to check myself before I say those words out loud.

My friends all stare at me—almost like they know what I'm about to say before I say it.

I gulp again. The crew is going to find out one way or the other. If I don't tell them, John will.

"Andy sabotaged Carter's SCBA. He had to take it off during the call. He couldn't breathe."

They all gasp and stare at me in horror. "You can NOT be serious!" Josh whispers. "He did NOT!"

I nod. "John has security camera footage from the firehouse showing Andy tampering with the SCBA last night while everyone was asleep."

"You mean...." Billy stammers. "Are you saying Andy actually snuck into the firehouse in the middle of the night—when he wasn't even rostered on shift—just so he could......?" He doesn't finish.

"He tried to kill Carter," Keith finishes. "That's all there is to it."

"John says Andy is downtown getting questioned by the Police," I finish. "That's why Carter had such bad smoke inhalation and respiratory burns. He had to take his mask off and his tank exploded at the same time."

Josh shakes his head. "Jesus! I have never heard anything as bad as that."

"That means Carter pulled Andy to safety without his mask on," Brooke murmurs. "Carter went through all that without a working SCBA and he still saved Andy's life."

"Yeah," I croak. "That's what happened."

The others glance toward the door. "Wow!" Chris breathes. "That is some first-class heroics right there."

"We all knew Carter was something special," Josh murmurs. "Now we all know it's true."

Brooke comes toward me and hugs me. "He's gonna pull through, sweetie. He's too tough to let something like this stop him."

My throat hurts. I can't speak.

Brooke backs off and then Josh hugs me. "We're all pulling for Carter. As soon as he gets out of here, he'll be back on duty and everything will go on as before."

"At least we won't have to deal with that snake again," Keith snarls. "John will never let him come back to the firehouse after this."

"If he doesn't wind up in prison first, you mean," Billy counters. "That's where he belongs—the traitorous bastard."

Chris nudges him. "Sophie doesn't need to hear you talking like that. She has enough to worry about."

Their conversation trails off and we all settle down to wait. I sink back into the same chair.

I'm just about to go back to staring at the wall when the others start talking amongst themselves.

They relate other details from the same call. These people around me right now are the ones who responded to the call with Carter.

These were the people who pulled him out of the burning house, gave him medical treatment, and transported him here.

Brooke was the one who intubated him and Josh treated his other injuries and broken arm.

I've never been more grateful for the firehouse family. Now they're sitting around supporting me, comforting me, and waiting for news just like I am.

Whatever happens to me, I won't have to go through it alone. These people admire Carter as much as I do.

They don't love him like I do. They don't know about our secret past together or our plans for the future.

Those are private secrets between me and Dylan. We just have to get through this. Then he'll come home to me and everything will happen the way we both dream it will.

I have to keep holding onto that. I can't survive this if I believe anything else.

Chapter 29:
Sophie

S omeone shakes me awake by the shoulder. "Sophie!" a woman whispers in my ear. "Sophie—wake up!"

I jolt out of a sound sleep and realize I'm still in the ICU waiting room. Ellen Foreman bends over me.

"It's time, Sophie," she murmurs. "The doctors extubated Carter. He's waking up. You should go see him."

I scramble to my feet, rub the sleep out of my eyes, and try to straighten my hair as best I can on my way down the hall.

Ellen escorts me as far as Carter's room and leaves me there. A few nurses surround his bed, but the doctors aren't here anymore.

Carter looks much more normal without the nasal tube and the ET tube blocking his face.

He lies on the bed with his eyes closed. He still looks drawn and weak, but he's back. He can breathe on his own, and while I stand there watching, he turns his head from one side to the other.

He doesn't look so much like a burn victim. He just looks like the man I love.

He doesn't see me when I step into the room and approach his bed. He sighs deeply and shudders when he lets out his breath.

I pick up his hand from the mattress next to him. He feels warm the way I remember.

He opens his eyes instantly and turns to look up at me. He frowns slightly when he focuses on me and then he shuts his eyes with a massive sigh of relief. "Thank God you're all right," he husks. "I've been going crazy about you."

I blink back tears at the sight of him. "You don't have to worry about me. I'm fine. You're the one we're all worried about."

"I'm okay," he croaks. "I mean...I will be as soon as I get out of here."

I have to smile at him. He's still too weak even to lift his arm. His fingers respond to my touch, but he doesn't take any of the weight of his arm when I pick it up.

"How do you feel?" I ask.

"Awful," he whispers. "Everything hurts. It hurts to breathe."

"You got respiratory burns and smoke inhalation when you took off your SCBA."

"I know," he rasps. "I had to. The hoses failed."

I don't tell him the rest. He'll find out soon enough, too.

I pet the back of his hand and feel the scars I love so much. I would touch the rest of him, but I don't want to hurt him.

"I love you, Dylan," I whisper.

"I love you so much, baby!" His voice spikes with tormented strain. "I don't want anything but to come home to you at the end of the day. I couldn't think about anything but you. You don't know how much I love you and need you." His eyes float up to mine. "Marry me, Sophie—please! I can't live without you. I never want to live without you again."

Tears well up in my eyes and spill down my cheeks. "Yes! I would give anything to marry you!"

He tries once to lift his arm and to pick his head up off the pillow. "Kiss me—please. I need to feel you touching me."

I bend over, kiss him very lightly, and stroke his cheeks. I don't want to hurt him, but I can feel that the doctors were telling the truth.

Carter's burns are no worse than they were before. He might have a few burns on his back, but his face, head, ears, and neck look and feel the same as I remember.

I don't stop touching his face when I sit back to gaze down at him.

He collapses into the pillow, shuts his eyes, and grimaces once when he tries to adjust his position in bed. Then he wilts and does his best not to move again.

"Tell me what's happening out there without me," he husks without opening his eyes. "Did the rest of the crew make it out okay?"

"Everyone is fine—everyone on the crew at least. The patients are in the hospital."

"Did Andy make it okay?" he asks.

I hesitate a second before I say, "He's fine. He got out without a scratch. You saved his life. Everyone is saying you're a hero."

"I just did my job," he croaks. "I couldn't leave him behind to die."

I take a deep breath. He wants to know what's happening out there. He better find out now before he hears it from someone else.

"John ran an arson screen on the house," I begin.

"It wasn't arson," he mutters. "The catering equipment blew up."

"I'm not talking about what caused the fire. Keith, Billy, Josh, and the other guys who pulled you out were concerned that you weren't wearing your SCBA. They could tell from the soot and blisters around your nose and mouth that you weren't wearing it through the whole call."

"I told you I had to take it off," he whispers. "The hoses failed and the explosion blew the regulator off my oxygen tank."

I gather my courage to say the next part. "The hoses didn't fail, Dylan—and the explosion didn't cause the regulator to blow. Andy tampered with your SCBA last night. He tried to kill you. He just didn't know that he would be the one you were in the middle of saving when it happened."

Carter's eyes snap open, but he doesn't move in any other way. He stares at the ceiling and his features harden.

"John found security camera footage from the firehouse," I finish. "The Police are questioning Andy now. We just haven't heard how he's going to answer the charges."

I wait for Carter to say something else. He can't exactly lose his temper when he's in this condition.

He stares at the ceiling in silence for a long time before he closes his eyes again. He settles back down in bed, compresses his lips only once, and doesn't show any other sign that he even knows about Andy's betrayal.

I sit on the edge of the bed and wait. I'm prepared to sit here in silence, too, for however long it takes him to be ready to talk to me.

He eventually mutters under his breath without opening his eyes, "I would do the same thing again—even knowing that."

I keep stroking the back of his hand. I want him to feel that I'm still here. He obviously needs that.

Of course he would do it again. Carter is the ultimate firefighter. He wouldn't leave any man in a burning building to die—not even a cold-blooded killer.

I would give just about anything to be a fly on the wall when Andy finds out what really happened in that building. I hope he realizes what a piece of shit he is.

None of that matters because I'm here with Carter and now I know he's going to be okay. He has to be okay if he's thinking this way.

I'm still sitting there hours later when some of the crew comes by. They're all wearing their uniforms, so a call must have brought them to the emergency room. Ellen comes with them and so does John.

They lurk around in the hallway waiting for permission to enter. Carter doesn't open his eyes when I put his hand down on the bed. He must be exhausted.

I go out into the hall. "Hey!" Ellen whispers. "How is he?"

"He's gonna be okay," I tell her and glance around the group to include everyone. "He's alert and talking. He's just really wiped out and in a lot of pain. He says it hurts to breathe, but he's thinking clearly." I glance up at John. "I told him about Andy."

"How did he take it?" Keith asks.

I try to shrug it away. "You know what Carter is like. He said he would do it again even knowing what he did."

"Jesus!" Billy breathes. "What an absolute badass!"

"Carter is worried about all of you," I go on. "He asked how all of you are doing."

"That on its own tells me he's going to be okay." John glances into the room. "Is he ready for visitors? We'll quietly disappear if he isn't."

"I'll ask him."

I go into the room, but when I take Carter's hand, he doesn't respond at all. He doesn't turn his head. His fingers lie unnaturally still in my grasp.

His chest rises and falls in a steady tide of sleep. A peaceful halo surrounds him. He doesn't wake up or open his eyes.

I slip out of the room.

"He's sleeping right now," I tell everyone. "He's really weak and tired. Maybe come back later."

"No problem," John replies. "Tell him we stopped by and we're all pulling for him."

"Thanks." I step forward and hug everyone one person at a time. "Thank you all for coming by. I know your support means a lot to him."

"Just let him know that Andy won't ever be coming back to the firehouse," John tells me. "Tell Carter he'll never have to put up with that jackass again."

"And neither will the rest of us," Keith growls. "It can't come soon enough."

I smile at everyone until they file away around the corner on their way back to work.

Their support means a lot to Carter, but it means even more to me. I wouldn't want him attending any call with any other crew. These people are pure gold.

I tiptoe back into the room and sit down in the chair next to Carter's bed. I don't take his hand again. I just stare at the side of his face while he sleeps. I want to be the first person he sees when he wakes up

.

Chapter 30: Carter

I groan when I heave myself out of my hospital bed. I'm being released today, but I feel like a wet rag.

The back side of my body aches every time I move. The bruises penetrate all the way to the bone.

Thank the stars in Heaven I didn't break any bones back there. I would have been laid up for months.

It's already been a week and I can barely move. Having my left arm in a sling is bad enough and my head throbs.

I still struggle to breathe even though the doctors say my lungs are healthy enough for me to leave the hospital. I'm out of the woods, but I'm still going to be recovering at home for at least another two weeks before I can go back to work.

I don't have to worry about that because Sophie never leaves my side. She goes around the room gathering what few personal items I've collected since I've been stuck in this place.

No one has told me what's happening with Andy and I haven't asked. He's either already in jail for attempted murder or he's under indictment for it.

I never want to hear the cocksucker's name again—and I don't have to. He's out of my life for good. Now I can concentrate on getting hurt the old-fashioned way—by the regular hazards of my job.

I don't envy the Health and Safety officer who has to audit this job after me. I'm the victim here. I don't have to do anything except piss and whine every time I move my good arm.

Sophie comes over to me and helps me get into a clean T-shirt and my pajama pants so I can ride home to my own bed.

The doctors have left my broken arm bandaged instead of putting my whole damn chest in plaster—thank God.

They say the plaster would aggravate the burns on my back. I don't care why as long as they don't plaster me. Anything would be better than that.

She takes my sling off, slips the T-shirt sleeve up my arm over the bandages, and twists and stretches the rest of the shirt over my head and body.

She wraps a jacket around my shoulder and I'm good to go except for my pants.

I have to stop multiple times to rest and catch my breath. I get winded from the tiniest exertion.

I barely manage to swivel into the wheelchair so the nurses can wheel me out to the truck. Sophie is driving me home in the truck because it's easier for me to get into the passenger seat.

I keep my eyes closed and rest on the way home. I still have to walk from the truck to the elevator and from the elevator to the apartment.

That's the longest I will have stayed on my feet since the accident. I'm still not sure I'll be able to make it, but I'll just have to. I don't want to spend my recovery sitting in the passenger seat of my truck.

She parks, takes my bag of personal effects out of the back, and opens my door for me.

She hovers around me, but fortunately for my sanity, she doesn't try to help me. She shuts the door and I hobble like an old man into the apartment complex.

I have to stop, lean against the wall, and catch my breath before I can make it to the elevator. Once I get inside, I lean against the railing to hold myself up. I never want to get smoke inhalation or respiratory burns ever again.

I stop three times on the way to the apartment. Maybe I should have taken the nurses up on their offer and brought home a wheelchair.

I won't need it once I get into the apartment. I just have to get there.

Sophie unlocks the door for me.

I could collapse on the couch, but that would mean another trek to the bedroom. I can't face that.

I go straight there and let my knees buckle. I sit down on the edge of the bed panting hard. Never again.

Sophie goes through the room straightening everything out even though it looks immaculate. She's been staying here while I've been in the hospital and she puts her apartment up for sale.

She sure takes care of the place. I don't see a single speck of dust anywhere.

She comes over to me and starts pulling down the covers so I can lie down.

"Would you please hand me that bag of personal effects, baby?" I ask.

I point to it and she brings it over to me. She doesn't tell me to move so she can pull the covers the rest of the way down.

She goes out to the kitchen and I hear her messing around in there. I rummage in my bag searching for something.

She comes back with a glass and a pitcher of water and sets both on the bedside table next to me. "What are you looking for?" she asks.

"This." I pull a crumpled brown paper bag out of the bottom of the bag.

She glances over. "What is it?"

I look up, take her hand, and pull her toward me. She's still standing up while I sit on the bed.

"Sophie McNish, would you please do me the honor of becoming my wife?" I ask.

I take that moment to pull the ring out of the paper bag. I only have one hand, so I have to slip the ring on her finger while she holds her hand out in front of me.

Her eyes fall out of their sockets when she sees the ring. "Where did you get that?!" she practically shrieks. Her face goes through a rapid series of transformations. "We were only together for two days before you got hurt—and you've been in the hospital ever since! You proposed to me after you regained consciousness! Where did you get this?!"

I have to smile at her. She's too smart for her own good. "I ordered it online when I was in the hospital. I had a phone. I hid the ring from you so I could propose to you the right way after we got home." I cock my head to study her. "So? Will you marry me?"

"Of course! I already said yes! How many times do I have to say it?!"

"I wanted to give you this. I didn't want our proposal to be in a hospital bed. I wanted it to be romantic enough for you."

"What's more romantic than that?!" She glances down at the ring and all the color drains out of her face when she stares at it.

I take in the effect of my surprise. Good. She's properly surprised and impressed by the ring.

I kiss her hand to get her attention. "I love you more than anything. I'm never going to let you go—not ever."

Her eyes dart up to me and her face transforms. Tears spring to her eyes and her mouth screws up in a twisted line before she attacks me.

She throws her arms around me, kisses me, and then hugs me hard enough to hurt me. "I love you so much, Dylan! I'm so happy! I can't believe I could ever be this happy."

She pushes me back, but everything she does sends blasts of agony shooting through me.

I don't have the heart to stop her when she holds me at arm's length. "I'm going to make you the happiest husband on the planet!" she tells me. "I'm going to do everything for you! You're never going to have to worry about anything! I promise."

I find myself laughing at her. "I'm sure whatever you do will be wonderful. You're already making me the happiest guy alive."

She breaks me in half with another impulsive hug, kisses me way too hard, and races away back to the kitchen. "Are you hungry? I can make you lunch if you are."

"Thank you," I mumble and topple onto the bed.

I don't even make it under the covers. I must have drifted off again, because when I wake up, it's evening. The sun is going down and a plate with a giant sandwich, a scoop of potato salad, a fork, and a napkin sit on the bedside table next to me.

Sophie isn't here, but I sense her somewhere in the apartment.

I drag myself to the pillow, prop myself up just enough to feed myself, drink a glass of water, and then crawl under the covers before I completely buckle again.

I'm just about to pass out again when Sophie comes in. "Oh, good. You got something to eat. Do you want anything else? Here. I brought you your phone."

She puts it on the bedside table next to me and takes the dishes to the kitchen. I hear her cleaning up and putting everything away.

I pick up my phone and check my emails. That's as strenuous as my life gets these days.

I read and respond to a metric crap-ton of messages from everyone on the firehouse crew wishing me well, telling me they're pulling for me, and asking if I need anything.

They also wish Sophie well and tell me to tell her that they can't wait for her to come back to work.

I work my way down the list until I get to another email from Emerson Freeman, my former supervisor at the Health and Safety Commission. If he's writing to ask me to come back, he's going to be sadly disappointed.

Nothing can prepare me for what I read.

I just got a call from Howe Fire Chief John Brewer about your accident and the subsequent criminal charges against Andrew Skinner. I just want to offer you my sincere well wishes for your recovery. You were always an outstanding firefighter and an even better Health and Safety officer.

The Commission has hired another up-and-coming firefighter to fill your vacancy. He's a go-getter and very enthusiastic about the job.

We were wondering if we could offer you a supervisory role in the Commission to manage him and four other inspection officers who will be auditing all the firehouses and Police Departments in the state.

You would be able to continue to live in Howe and work out of the same firehouse. You would even be able to continue working in the field if you want to. I know that's important to you and that your heart is in frontline emergency work.

We really need you and there would be a significant salary upgrade with the new position. It would also mean you would be able to transition out of frontline work when you get too old for that—which happens to the best of us, my friend.

Think about it. Chief Brewer said you were settling down with a girl up there, so leveling up your career is going to become more important in the years ahead. You won't be able to do frontline work forever and you won't want to risk another injury like this once you have a family to think about.

We would love it if you accepted this position. Please let me know how you feel about that. I can send you any information you need to help you make your decision.

I can't think of anyone better qualified to teach these new officers how to conduct their audits the right way.

I can also assure you that there would be no conflict of interest with you supervising the officers who will be auditing Howe Fire Department. You'll only be leading the officers who will be auditing the department instead of auditing it yourself—so you can put that concern to rest.

The Commission is extremely anxious to keep you on, my friend. We don't want to lose you just because your life is changing. Let me know what you think. I won't be waiting by the phone for you to answer. Take your time and don't feel any rush to come to a decision before you recover from your injuries.

I'm thinking of you and wishing you all the best.

Sincerely,

Emerson Freeman

I'm still staring at the phone in shocked disbelief when Sophie comes back. I even forget to look at her when she changes into her pajamas and slips into bed next to me.

I stare at the ceiling taking it all in. This is amazing.

It almost feels like the world is rolling out the red carpet in front of me and leading me to the life of my dreams.

He's right. I won't be able to take these risks when I have a wife and a bunch of kids to take care of.

One of these days, I'll need to transition out of emergency work and take the remote equivalent of a desk job.

Sophie doesn't snuggle in right away. She's lying on the same side as my broken arm, so she's probably worried about hurting me.

I don't know how much good I'm going to be to her in the next couple of days, but I want her near me—as near as I can handle.

I put the phone on the bedside table and switch off the lamp. The apartment and the rest of the world fall into darkness.

I'm going to have to take plenty of time to think about that email before I decide how I respond.

Oh, who am I kidding? I already know I'll take the position. This is exactly what I need.

Sophie still keeps her distance when I sink down on the pillow. I don't want her lying over there at a distance from me.

"Come around the other side of the bed so I can hold you, baby," I murmur in the dark. "Don't stay over there."

She leans in and kisses me before she climbs out and walks around the bed to get in on my other side.

"This doesn't feel right," she whispers. "This feels all wrong."

"It's temporary," I tell her and pull her toward me, but that doesn't feel right, either.

I scoot down the bed, wrap my one good arm around her waist, and pull her all the way in so I can bury my face in her breasts through her soft, cotton tank top.

She kisses the top of my head and wraps her arms around my head to hug me into her, but that's all. I don't have the energy to do anything but fall asleep here.

I don't have to do anything else. I'm where I belong and no one expects anything else from me.

Chapter 31:
Carter

I park my truck, shift it into *Park* with one hand, and climb out. I still have my arm in a sling and I walk hitched over on one side. My body still doesn't work right after all the soft tissue injuries, but I'm getting better.

I limp into the firehouse and the crew bursts into cheers when they see me. They all surround me laughing, clapping me on the back way too hard, making a big noise, and bombarding me with questions.

I can't hear anything over the noise. I can only stand here and smile at them all. It sure is nice to belong somewhere.

"Did you hear Andy is fighting the attempted murder charge?" Ellis asks me.

"Yeah, I heard. The guy doesn't know when to give up."

"I don't know how a guy could go so wrong," Billy remarks. "He wasn't that bad to begin with. He wasn't the greatest, but he wasn't the worst, either. Who knew he could fall so far?"

"When do you think you'll get back on the job?" Josh asks me.

"Not until my arm heals up at the earliest," I reply. "Sophie will be coming back next week, though. She's climbing the walls at home with just me to look at."

They laugh. "I'm surprised she lasted this long," Chris tells me. "She must really love you."

I feel my skin burning, but just then, Chief Brewer rolls in and passes us on his way to the stairs.

I shoot the breeze with the crew for a little while. I get distracted when Danny comes in. He isn't walking on crutches anymore nor does he wear a brace, but he still limps.

He grins when he sees me. "Hey, it's my evil twin! You're gonna start making me feel bad for staying away for so long."

"It's a good thing you're coming back now," Keith tells him. "Our crewmates are dropping like flies. We need everyone on deck."

"I'll get back as soon as I can," I reply.

"I'm not talking about you!" he counters. "You shouldn't even be here. Look at you, man! You can barely stand up."

I can't stop laughing. "Watch it! I'm not that bad. I have a broken arm. That's all."

"Oh, really? Run over there and climb into the truck. I double-dog dare you."

I don't move. "Hell no!"

Everybody laughs. "You see?" Keith waves at me. "Get outta here, fool!"

We laugh some more, but I feel my destiny calling me.

"I gotta go upstairs and talk to the man," I tell the others. "Don't you people have some trucks to check?"

"Listen to this guy!" Danny exclaims. "He got busted down to firefighter and he still thinks he can tell us what to do!"

They laugh, break up, and head for their trucks while I hobble over to the stairs.

"Hey!" Josh yells after me. "We're going out for drinks tonight. You and Sophie should come with us—if your liver can stand it."

"Forget about your liver," Caleb adds. "Bring an extra pair of eardrums while you're at it."

I grin at them all before I pass through the door. "We'd love to come. Thanks for the invitation."

I take extra long limping up the stairs. I finally make it to Chief Brewer's office.

He looks up in surprise and then smirks when I walk in. "Hey! Look what the cat dragged in."

I make a face. "Very funny."

He stops smiling when I shut the door. "You okay?" he asks. "I mean—apart from the obvious?" He frowns. "Is something wrong?"

I sit down in the chair across his desk. I don't want to stand up anymore. "Sophie and I are getting married. I just wanted you to be the first to hear it from me."

He bursts into another grin. "Congratulations. I'm happy for both of you. You deserve each other. You're both really good for each other."

"I also want you to know that I got offered a supervisor's position with the Health and Safety Commission. I'll be managing and leading five other inspection officers all over the state, but I'll be doing it remotely from Howe. I'll be able to keep working in the field for now—once I come back on duty. I don't anticipate the two roles conflicting with each other—not yet anyway."

"That's great," he exclaims. "This will be perfect for you."

I blink at him. "You're cool with this? You don't have a problem with the firehouse being my part-time job?"

He laughs. "I'm cool with any job that keeps you here. You're part of the family now, and frankly, I can't run this place without you. I'll keep you on as long as I can—no questions asked."

I have to look away. "Thanks. This place is pretty special."

He won't stop beaming at me. "So are you. You're a hero to all of us. You belong here."

I feel my face burning again. "Thanks. I feel that way, too."

He waits for me to say something else. "Is that all you wanted to tell me?"

"No...just.....thanks.....for everything. Thank you for always backing me up. I never thought I'd ever find someplace like this."

He turns back to his work. "Well, you found it. It must have been meant to be."

I can only murmur, "Yeah," and slip out of his office. It really was meant to be.

The crew is all buried up to their eyeballs in their truck and equipment checks when I get back down to the garage. I wave goodbye to them and we agree to meet up that evening.

I drive home and find Sophie sitting in front of her laptop staring at the screen. "You just checked the real estate listings this morning," I tell her. "Things don't change that fast around here."

"I know!" she groans. "I seem to be obsessed with this business of finding the perfect house."

I fall onto the couch. "You need to go back to work. You have way too much time on your hands."

"That won't help, either. What do you think I'll be doing while we're all sitting around in the breakroom shooting our mouths off? I'll be glued to my phone."

"We can live in this apartment for as long as it takes to find a house," I tell her. "We can even live here after the baby is born."

She shoots me a smirk over my shoulder. "What baby is that?"

I look away. "I'm just saying. Besides, the crew invited us to go out for drinks tonight. That will take your mind off it."

She looks up and her eyes widen. "They did? That's awesome!"

"Are you sure you want to go out in public with Quasimodo?"

She makes a face. "Don't call yourself that. You're the hottest man alive as far as I'm concerned."

She turns back to the computer. I study her across the living room. She's by far the hottest woman alive as far as I'm concerned.

I want her, but I have to be careful about how I do it so I don't hurt myself. She would be more than accommodating, but I don't want to disturb her.

She only scrolls on the real estate website for a minute before she jerks around in her chair and narrows her eyes at me. "You're thinking about it again."

I glance left and right. "I'm thinking about what again? I wasn't thinking about anything."

"You're lying. You were thinking about sex."

I blink at her in mock surprise. "Me? I don't think about sex. I have way more important things to think about....like how beautiful you are."

"I know you, remember? I can tell when you're looking at me like that."

She leaves her laptop open and saunters toward me. She's wearing her pajama pants and a regular T-shirt—with a bra under it this time.

I pretend she isn't coming toward me for that, but I can't pretend anymore when she pushes me back on the couch cushions, slips out of her clothes, and straddles me.

I can only touch her with one hand, but her intentions couldn't be more obvious. She wants me to.

I enjoy myself playing with her breasts, following all her curves, and pulling her ass forward so she rides me and feels how hard I'm getting.

She's been taking good care of me since I've been stuck at home. She never leaves me wanting even if she has to be gentle with me.

I don't have to do anything but lie here and watch her majestic body swaying on my lap. Her hips arch so deliciously when she flexes her ass forward and then back to grind on my package.

Her cheeks color and her breath quickens as her eyes glaze over.

"So beautiful!" I whisper as I stroke my hand down her perfect skin to the point between her thighs.

Just because, I slip my fingers into her wetness so I can feel her closing around me. This is how she'll close around me just as soon as she unzips me to take me inside.

She throws back her head in a husky moan when she grinds into my hand. I get a handful of hot, sweet, slippery juice when she pumps my fingers all the way in and then starts rocking for the moon.

She leans all the way forward and shoves her breasts in my face the way she knows I like it the best.

She throws her head all the way back and her moans rise to screams as I devour her nipples. Her screams flood my brain.

She loses the sense of trying to be gentle with me, grabs my head, and pulls me harder into her chest. This position skyrockets her out of this world and she climaxes again and again on my hand.

I sink into a daze of pure bliss feeling her body spasm and thrash on my hand. I would like to hold onto her with my other arm, but I can't move it.

That doesn't stop her, though, and in a minute, she pulls her chest back so she can kiss me.

I catch a split second's view of her smoky, sex-drugged eyes. She stares at something beyond time before her mouth closes on me.

She eventually pulls herself off my fingers and collapses sobbing on my shoulder. Her body smells heavenly and her skin feels extra soft after she let herself go like that.

I love the way she gets all floppy and glowing after I make her climax—preferably many times. She melts into me and huddles on my shoulder still mewing and sighing as the energy dwindles.

I kiss the side of her head, stroke her hair, and go back to admiring every curve and swoop of her body.

Touching her turns her on again. She stiffens when I play with her breasts or squeeze her ass and thighs.

Her moans change their sound and she pants against my neck. I could wind her up again and I probably will.

Before I think to start, she slides down me, drops on her knees in front of me, and burrows her face into my package. She nibbles me through my jeans and her hands migrate to my fly.

I strip it open for her and her mouth closes on me. The sensation floods me with so much pleasure that I can't help but grab her hair and growl at her.

She dissolves in my grip. I love the feeling of her releasing herself to me.

Her mouth consumes me beyond my wildest dreams. She doesn't stop until she leaves me gasping, panting, and roaring in fulfillment.

Now I'm the one who loses the sense of being gentle. I forget what I'm doing and thrust into her mouth. I can't stop the floodgates from opening, but even doing it like this doesn't satisfy me.

As soon as I finish, she wraps her arms around my waist and hugs me there. She might be fragile after just having her own orgasm, but I'm just getting started.

I pull her up and kiss her. "Lean back on the table, baby. Let me taste some of your sweetness."

She obeys instantly and sits back on the coffee table all naked and beautiful.

Her eyes lock on me when she leans back, props herself on her elbows, and spreads her legs for me.

She watches me in smoldering passion as I shift onto my knees on the floor. She watches me all the way down when I bury my head between her legs and fall into a dark abyss of heavenly rapture.

Her flesh blasts my mind into so many cosmic dimensions of pleasure and happiness.

I hear her screaming and shoving herself against me when I lick her to another blistering climax. She flies completely off the charts when I stab my fingers inside and start drilling her.

She falls back on the table, raises her arms above her head, and arches into my hand and face. Her screams echo through the apartment again and again.

Her taste and smell intoxicate me. Her screams, sobs, and cries become the most beautiful symphony I've ever heard.

I could stay down here for days and never get tired of this, but the painful throbbing hardness of my shaft distracts me. Her mouth makes me harder and hotter to take her for real.

My shaft has another agenda in mind. My shaft wants to pump my seed into her and fill her up with new life. All the rest of this enjoyment is just a prelude to that.

I pull out of her thighs, rise up on my knees, and look down at her body undulating and convulsing in front of me.

She locks her hands behind her head and crunches forward in time to my fingers filling her channel. Then she arches back to throw her breasts into the air.

Her thighs widen into a perfect hourglass just waiting for me to move between her legs.

She's already lying right in front of my hips. It takes no effort at all to withdraw my fingers and lean into her instead.

She arches all the way back when I do and immediately starts screaming even louder.

She extends her hands above her head, takes hold of the opposite edge of the coffee table, and bends her back all the way off the surface to take me inside her.

I want to grab her by the hips and pull her into my thrusts, but I can only do that with one hand. I plow deep into her darkest places. I want to get as deep as I can, but I can't get any deeper than this.

I even scoop my hand under her back to bring her in tight. She thrashes and sways in such beautiful curves. She angles her hips downward to meet me and then raises her thighs so my pelvis smacks her damp, succulent ass.

Her soft sweetness envelops me in magical rapture. I can't hold off any longer. This is the moment. Her fertile ground is ready for my seed. Her body practically begs me for it.

I lean forward against her thighs and prop my arm next to her head. "Look at me, baby," I rasp. "Look at me."

Her eyes float open, but I can't tell if she's even aware of me. I want her to see me when I plant my seed in her.

I know she sees me. I know she knows who this is that's conquering her body right now.

Her sex-crazed eyes lock on me and blaze with madness as I build up the last few seconds of brutal intensity. I want to touch her all over and even to bury my face in her flesh at the moment of climax, but that isn't possible.

Her face wrenches in all the wrong ways as she peaks again and again right in front of me. Her body has never been better prepared.

I drive in and my load explodes out of me beyond my control. Searing heat rushes through me from her channel as her deep darkness swallows every precious drop.

Her inner muscles milk me dry and the excess dribbles out around my shaft and down her ass.

Her eyes roll back in their sockets and she screams again and again when I pump it into her. Does she feel it? Does this turn her on as much as it turns me on?

She wraps her thighs around me and pulls me in tight while I shudder and pulsate to eject the last torturous bursts into her depths before we both collapse apart.

Chapter 32:
Sophie

I wake up to Carter nibbling across my chest, nuzzling my breasts, and then his insatiable mouth clamps on my nipples. I moan half asleep as he starts to suck.

I feel myself spiraling out of control again when he slips his fingers between my legs. He can feel how swollen and sopping I still am from our encounter in the living room.

I whine and then start to cry out in rising tension as he fingers me, but he stops before I can wind all the way up to another climax.

His constant attention keeps me hovering on the brink of climax all the time. He never leaves enough time for me to come down before he sends me reeling over the edge into another one.

Before I can really explode, he pulls away, pushes me onto my back, and plunges his face between my legs. His burrowing tongue and big, juicy bites launch me into another dizzy spiral.

I spread my legs wide to take him in, but he stops that after just a few delirious seconds.

He falls back on the bed with a heavy sigh. "We should get ready to go out, baby."

I groan and roll over to cuddle against him. He's still fully dressed. He hasn't taken his clothes off since he came home from the firehouse.

I don't think I can face going out with the fire crew—not after he reduced me to a quivering wreck.

I just want to crawl inside him and disappear. I don't want to face the world right now, but I have to. I'll be going back to work tomorrow.

He leans over and kisses me on the forehead. "Come on, baby. We need to get out of this apartment at least for one night. We've been locked up in here for weeks. Come on. Get up, take a shower, and get dressed. We're going out tonight."

I groan again, but he's right. Hiding from the world never works.

I know he's been getting antsy from having to stay in the apartment all the time. He needs to get out as much as I do.

I drag myself off to the shower, but I have to be careful when it comes to soaping myself up. Touching myself turns me on again. I have to be careful that I don't wind up staying in here too long pleasuring myself when I'm supposed to be functioning—or pretending to.

Carter gives me a look when I come out—almost like he knows what I've been doing.

He can always sense when I'm feeling sexual—the same way I can sense when he's fantasizing about me and planning to do something with me. It's a kind of telepathy between us that always leads to us fooling around.

I somehow manage to get dressed and do my hair and makeup. I decide to do something nice for Carter by wearing the dress I wore to the bowling alley. I know he likes that one.

His eyes go hard and trace up and down my body when he sees me wearing it. He compresses his lips and forces himself to look away, but I already know what he's thinking.

I know what we'll be doing tonight after we get home from spending time with our friends.

He dresses up his usual casual T-shirt and jeans by putting on a blazer over them. I help him slip his jacket over his arm and then put his sling back on.

He kisses me when we leave the apartment, but he keeps it short and sweet before he escorts me out to his truck. He puts me in the passenger seat and drives us into town.

We walk into a bustling, noisy bar packed with people.

We meet up with Brooke, Billy, Chris, Josh, Keith, Leila, Danny, Emily, Caleb, Ellis, Jessie, Naomi, Vince, Drew, and George already waiting for us there.

Carter goes to the bar to get our drinks. The guys hug me, tell me how great it is to see me again after so long, and then the women all surround me.

"So when are you going to set a date?" Brooke asks me.

"We already did," I tell her. "It's four months from now on Memorial Day. We figure more people will have the day off then."

"Where are you doing it?" Chris asks. "Are you going to get married in a big church and all that?"

"Naw. Neither of us wants that. We want to have a small firehouse ceremony like you and Josh did—but without the psycho exes turning up to spoil everything."

She laughs. "Good idea. Skip that part."

"Do you have your dress picked out yet?" Emily asks. "Let me know if you need any help planning the decorations and food and everything else."

"That's the problem. I get so obsessed with trying to find a house for us to move into. I don't seem to be able to concentrate on the wedding at all."

"You better concentrate on it," Leila tells me. "Four months is nothing. It will be here before you know it."

"I know!" I exclaim. "I sit down in front of my laptop to organize the wedding, but I always wind up back on the real estate sites instead."

"Are you finding anything promising?" Brooke asks.

"Not really. Carter keeps telling me we can stay in the apartment for as long as we need to, but for some reason, this idea of buying a house seems to take over my brain. I don't seem to be able to think about anything else."

"Maybe you should let him handle buying the house while you deal with the wedding. Make a pact with him that you won't look at the real estate sites ever again. He can let you know when he finds a promising house and he can take you to see it, but you remove yourself from the search process completely and just trust him to handle it."

I gape at her in horror. "Are you serious?! You mean—like—just let him choose the house—by himself?!"

She laughs at me. "No, silly. You would both choose the house, but he can be responsible for searching the real estate sites and letting you know when he finds something good. I'm sure he knows by now what you want. Doesn't he? He's a grown man. He knows how to use the internet."

I shut my mouth in a hurry. I really must be addicted to this house hunt thing if I can't even trust Carter to check the real estate websites for me.

Just then, Carter comes back with our drinks, hands me mine, and inclines his head to one side. "We're going to get a table. Come on."

The other women and I follow as the guys plow through the mob toward the back of the bar. There are a lot of people here.

The crowd jostles us and winds up cutting between us and the guys. Right then, a group of loud, rowdy guys bumps into us, shoves me and the other women into a tighter group, and some of the strangers block us from catching up with the men.

I pull back and raise my glass so I don't spill my drink. Four of the strangers notice me and turn around to face me. "Sorry about that!" one of them calls out and then immediately changes his tone when he sees me. "Hey, baby! Are you here alone? Come over to our table and join us."

"Thanks, but I'm not here alone. Excuse me."

I try unsuccessfully both to back away from him and to step forward to walk around him. I can't do either. Too many people cut me off in front and behind.

I can't even see the guys anymore with so many people in the way. Even the women seem to have disappeared into the crowd.

I cast a desperate look around and see Naomi disappearing into the crowd. I'm all alone here.

The four guys who bumped into me move in for the kill. They surround me in a ring and the one who invited me to his table actually puts his arm around my waist.

"You aren't really here alone, are you, baby?" he purrs. "Come on. Don't play hard to get."

I'm just trying to decide if I should throw my drink at him or kick him in the nuts when Carter appears out of nowhere, shoves us apart, and steps in front of me.

I could throw my arms around him for showing up like this, but the tension in his shoulders tells me not to touch him.

He holds his one good arm out in front of him to steer the other guys away. "Back off, fellas," he tells the strangers. "She told you she isn't interested. Now go back to your table and leave her alone."

The strangers take one look at his burned face and his arm in the sling and sneer at him. "Who the hell are you—her demon consort?"

The first guy bursts out in cruel laughter. "You don't belong in the same county as a woman this fine, you freak."

Carter narrows his eyes at them. Don't ask me what he'll do with one broken arm and the rest of his body already beaten to a pulp.

"What I look like doesn't mean squat, pal," he mutters. "She said she wasn't interested. You should know better than to go around putting your hands on strange women in public places. Now walk away before you wind up doing something you regret."

"What are you going to do to stop me?" The first guy barges up to Carter and tries to chest-bump him. The guy deliberately changes his angle of approach to bump Carter's broken arm instead. "No way can you convince me a fox like that is out here with you."

Carter grits his teeth, probably to tell these idiots for the second time that it doesn't matter if I'm out with him because I already said I wasn't interested in going anywhere with these guys.

I don't even realize the firehouse guys are here before Billy steps in. He's so much bigger than every other man in the building.

He doesn't have to say a word. He shoves between Carter and the would-be assailant, swells up his bulky shoulders, and creates a physical barrier between Carter and the four strangers.

Like magic, Keith shows up at the same time and plants himself on Billy's other side. Keith and Billy form a wall of muscle so big and solid that the strangers probably can't even see Carter anymore.

Danny, Ellis, Josh, Caleb, Vince, Drew, and George surround the party at the same time.

"You mess with him, you mess with all of us," Keith snarls through gritted teeth. "Do yourselves a favor and walk away with your dignity intact."

The four strangers glare at the firehouse guys and then pull each other away. They vanish into the crowd and the tension dissolves.

The firehouse guys take longer to power down. They keep shooting death glares at everyone around us, but no one challenges us.

Then the guys turn around and surround Carter. "You okay?" Keith asks.

"I'm fine," he murmurs. "Thanks for that."

"No one messes with one of ours," Billy growls. "Come on. Let's go."

He and the other guys sweep me into the middle of the pack. They stay with me this time and escort me and Carter back to their table.

I slide into the seat with the other women and Carter wedges himself in next to me. He has to hug his arm close to his chest so it doesn't bump against the table.

I want to ask if that guy hurt Carter's arm, but I don't want to say anything in front of the crew.

Everyone starts talking at once. The flow of conversation wipes out what just happened.

In a minute, Ellis raises his glass. "Here's to Carter and Sophie. May you have a long, happy, prosperous future together."

Everyone joins in the toast and we all drink before the conversation starts up again. I glance over at Carter at the same moment he glances over at me. We're with family here. Life has never been better.

Chapter 33: Sophie

I park Carter's pickup in the beach parking lot and wave to John, Ellen, and a bunch of the off-duty crew. They're already down there setting up for the barbecue.

I switch off the motor and pull down the tailgate, but before I can take out the coolers, the rescue truck pulls into the parking lot behind me.

"Don't you dare try to lift that!" Carter tells me through the open window. "You're making me look bad."

I laugh at him and wait for Keith to turn the truck backward and park before the crew unloads.

Carter comes over and takes one of the coolers. His arm is all healed now and he's been back at work for a week.

No one would ever know he ever gotten injured. He kisses me once and heads off down the beach carrying the cooler easily.

Keith and Billy take the other two coolers off my hands. "Now I have nothing to do," I pretend to complain.

Brooke and Chris laugh and flank me on our way down the beach. We join the flow of jokes, snide remarks, and stories from our recent calls.

"Are you gonna go surfing again today?" Chris asks Carter.

"I can't. I'm on duty," he tells her. "I might get a call when I'm out there with my head underwater. Then the whole crew would get delayed while I put my clothes back on."

"We would just leave without you," Keith adds.

"Like hell you would," Carter counters. "You're nowhere near as good at scaring the patients as I am."

They all laugh and we gather in a circle eating, drinking, and talking.

"I found a new paramedic to take Andy's place," John announces.

Groans and yells of protest answer him. "Not that again!" Caleb howls. "Who is it this time—Mrs. Doubtfire?"

Laughter breaks out.

"No, she's a trained paramedic," John tells us. "Her name is Allison and she's twenty-seven. She worked in Woodhurst for a few years, moved Back East, and now she's moving here."

"Is she from Howe?" Ellis asks.

"I don't know where she's from. I didn't ask. I was more concerned with her resume."

"So when is she going to start?" I ask.

"I haven't finished interviewing her, but she's promising. I have a good feeling about her. She has a good sense of humor and she has a cheery personality. I think she's going to fit in well here."

Billy rolls his eyes. "I'll believe it when I see it. She could be another flake like all the others."

"Give her a chance," John insists. "We got Josh, didn't we? There are still a few good people out there. We just have to find them."

"You hired twenty bad people before we got Josh," Brooke points out. "Twenty to one isn't very good odds."

"That doesn't mean we'll have to go through twenty more bad people before we find the next person who fits in with us. She could be it."

"We'll see about that," Billy grumbles.

"Don't make it harder for her than it already is," John insists. "Be nice to her and welcome her. Then, if it doesn't work out, it will be on her—not us. Make her see that we're all about family here. Make her see that this is the best place to work. She might take to it."

"It really is the best place to work," Carter chimes in. "This place is the best."

That breaks the tension again and people start talking about other stuff. Chris turns to me. "Well? When do we get to see the new house?"

"We're moving in the week before the wedding," I tell her. "We both want to go home from the wedding to the new house."

She puffs out her cheeks and raises her eyebrows. "You're adding moving on top of the wedding plans? You're insane!"

I laugh. "Yeah. I guess we are."

I'm just about to ask about her and Josh. I know they've been trying to get pregnant for a few months now.

I open my mouth when Brooke whispers in my ear. "Oh, no! Don't look!"

Of course I have to look. I turn around to see what she's talking about.

Silence falls over the barbecue when another car pulls into the beach parking lot. Andy gets out.

He doesn't look like a hardened criminal. He wears clean khaki slacks and a casual bomber jacket over his white T-shirt. He looks like the same guy we've been working with all these years.

I still find it hard to believe that he tried to kill Carter. Is Andy coming here to try to patch things up with all of us?

I don't see how that's possible, but maybe Andy finally came to his senses when he found out about Carter saving his life. Stranger things have happened.

Carter would be the first to offer an olive. The rest of us won't be so quick to forgive.

"What the hell is he doing here?" Billy snarls. "He should be in jail."

"He's out on bail until his case goes to trial," Chris murmurs.

"We have a restraining order against him," John snaps. "He isn't supposed to be within a hundred yards of Carter or any other fire-house employee."

"I'll handle this." Keith barges forward, but Andy is already striding down the beach heading straight for us with his hands in his jacket pockets.

He makes it almost all the way to us before Keith, Billy, George, and Drew step between Andy and the rest of us.

"You don't belong here, man," Keith rumbles. "Turn around and go back to your car. We have a restraining order against you. Leave now or we'll call the Police."

Andy's eyes trace the group. He doesn't seem to pay any particular attention to Carter.

Andy's gaze locks on me for a second. "I heard Carter and Sophie are getting married."

"That's none of your business," Billy snaps. "And don't even think about showing up to the wedding. You aren't welcome. There will be plenty of us on hand to throw you out if you decide to make trouble."

"I'm not trying to make trouble," Andy replies, but his eyes tell me otherwise. They keep skipping around everywhere. He doesn't look at anything for very long.

"What do you want?" Keith counters. "What the hell are you doing here? You aren't part of this anymore—if you ever were."

Andy doesn't seem to have an answer for that. He just stands there like he didn't hear Keith's question.

Andy keeps looking around at everyone and no one in particular.

Just as I predicted, Carter steps forward. He approaches Keith, Billy, George, and Drew from behind.

He starts to say, "Listen, man, I just want to say...."

Lightning quick, Andy pulls his hands out of his pockets the instant Carter comes within range. I catch one split-second view of a gun in his hand before he brings it up to level it at Carter's head.

I open my mouth to yell out a warning, but it's all over in an instant.

Keith, Billy, and the others dive for Andy, but not fast enough. The gun aims directly for Carter's head within a few feet away from his face.

Before anyone can move, a flying missile hurtles across the beach and Ellis tackles Carter out of the way.

They slam down onto the sand just as the gun goes off. The bullet flies past where Carter was just standing, hits John Brewer in the head instead, and he topples like a ton of bricks.

"JOHN!!" Ellen shrieks and charges forward as fast as she can on her leg brace.

Keith loses his grip on Andy to turn around and see his brother lying on the ground in a pool of blood.

Chris, Brooke, Leila, and I all rush in to surround John. We all freeze when we see him lying there with half his head blown off. He doesn't need a paramedic. No one can come back from this. There's no point in even trying.

Ellen rushes him, but she must realize the truth, too. She collapses on her knees next to him, grabs his uniform, and tries to pick him up. His weight falls back down into the same pool of blood-stained sand.

"JOHN!!" she shrieks. "JOHN!!"

Billy, George, Drew, and Caleb attack Andy, bring him to the ground, and I hear muffled thumps coming from behind me.

I can't move. I stand staring in mindless shock at the body on the ground. He can't be dead. He can't be.

Oakleigh comes over just then. She heads for the picnic table. She doesn't realize what's happening until she hears Ellen screaming.

Oakleigh rushes over and starts screaming, too. "DAD!! DADD!!"

She would attack the body, too, but Danny catches her, holds her back, and eventually has to lift her off the ground and restrain her.

She kicks and thrashes screaming and wailing in bitter tears. He hugs her in his arms and walks away with her down the beach.

I barely notice Ellis and Carter standing up. I don't see or hear anything until the Police sirens blast into the beach parking lot.

Josh, Chris, and Leila have to drag Ellen away from John's body as the Police swarm the beach. Billy, George, Drew, and Caleb sit on Andy and hold him down until the Police take him into custody.

Then it's all over but the crying as the Police mark off the whole damn beach, turn it into a crime scene, and go through the whole fire crew taking statements from everyone.

Danny doesn't come back with Oakleigh until the very last minute. Emily gives her statement and then takes Oakleigh to their car while Danny gives his statement.

He lurches through it in numb shock. The rest of the crew stands around staring down at the body while the Crime Lab people draw lines around the body and the gun.

They mark off the distance between John's body and where they find the bullet that exited his skull and flew twenty feet down the beach.

They treat his death as such a clinical science experiment. I know they have to do this, but this whole exercise seems like such an insult.

John Brewer is dead. This can't be real. He was a force of nature in this town. He meant as much to the Police force as he did to us. How can all these people just go on as if nothing happened?

The Brewers leave first. Danny and Emily take Zeke and Oakleigh home to their house. Then Keith and Leila leave with baby Leon. Keith and Leila don't say a word to anyone besides the Police before the two of them get in their car and drive away.

They leave a black hole of despair hanging over the beach. The other parents get their kids out of there as soon as the Police tell them they can go.

Ellen sits at the picnic table sobbing into her hands. Brooke and Naomi sit on either side of her. Caleb stands over them.

The rest of us just stare down at the body. That can't be John Brewer. Now what are the rest of us going to do without him? This crew can't function without him. He's everything that makes Howe Fire Department so great.

Carter comes over to me and puts his arm around my shoulder. "Let's get out of here," he murmurs in my ear.

I can't move. I can't speak or even look at him. I have to keep standing here watching while the Crime Lab people put John in a body bag and take him away.

They leave the outline on the sand, take a million pictures, and then Police Chief Jim Walker comes over to us. "We need to cordon off the crime scene now. We have to ask you all to leave. You can take your leftover food and coolers and the barbecue and everything. Just try not to disturb the crime scene any more than you have to."

I shake myself out of my trance and get to work. Brooke and Billy put Ellen in Brooke's car. Brooke drives Ellen away while Billy helps us load all the stuff into the remaining vehicles.

Almost all the coolers, barbecue, and most of the food winds up in the back of Carter's pickup. It's the only vehicle left that's big enough to carry it all.

None of us talks or even looks at each other. I do my best not to look at the crime scene again.

We don't try to sort the stuff out. The barbecue is Keith's. No way in hell will I take it back to his house now.

I'm just getting ready to drive away when Carter comes over to me. He moves his face in front of my eyes so I have no choice but to look at him.

"Are you going to be okay by yourself?" he murmurs. "You can come to the firehouse if you aren't."

I shrug and look away. "I'll be okay, I guess."

He kisses me on the forehead before he leaves to go back to the truck. Keith and Danny are both gone. That leaves the truck short-handed without two of the rostered firefighters.

Billy gets behind the wheel without a word. Carter, Caleb, Josh, and Chris load up in the back.

None of them even says goodbye before everyone drives off in different directions.

I don't allow myself to think about anything while I drive home and put everything away. I put the barbecue and the extra coolers in the storage room downstairs. Most of my stuff from my apartment is in there until Carter and move our combined stuff into our new house.

I put all the leftover food and drinks in the fridge. I don't know what else to do with this stuff, but I don't want to waste it. There's enough here to feed me and Carter for a month.

I have nothing else to do with the rest of the day and I really need to take my mind off everything that just happened. I can't start thinking about the fact that John Brewer is dead—and that Andy tried to kill Carter again right in front of all of us.

I go through the whole apartment and clean everything extra well just because. Then I clean Carter's truck and my car inside and out.

I'm just about to go back to my laptop and bury myself in the wedding plans. God only knows how Carter and I can get married now.

We won't be able to hold the wedding at the firehouse. That's out of the question.

I can't think where else we could hold it. We might have to settle for a small, private ceremony right here in the apartment.

Neither Carter nor I have told our families that we're getting married. Our families don't even know that Dylan and I found each other again. This is all going so fast.

I'll have to sit my parents down and have a discussion with them about what Dylan looks like before they see him again. I'll have to warn them about how bad he looks.

They'll be happy for me. They always liked Dylan and they know how much he means to me.

I go back inside and put away all my cleaning gear, but when I head for my desk, he comes home from the firehouse. I must have lost track of time.

He studies me extra closely. "Are you okay?"

I nod at nothing. "I'm all right. How is everyone else?"

"They're getting through the day and keeping the firehouse running. That's the best anyone can hope for right now."

"Has anyone heard from the Brewers?"

"No one has heard and no one has tried to contact them. I couldn't do it."

"No, I couldn't, either. I guess it will be a while before we hear anything from them."

He pulls me down on the couch next to him. "Come here, baby."

He doesn't say anything else. He puts his good arm around me, but he doesn't bury his face in my chest the way he usually does.

He wraps his arm around my shoulders and brings me into his chest. He hugs me there, kisses me on the head, and holds me against him.

I'm the one who needs comforting right now. I can barely function.

I shut my eyes and the truth hits me like a ton of bricks. John Brewer is dead.

I don't know how to be alive in a world where he isn't running Howe Firehouse. I don't see how the world can keep turning without him here.

How will Keith, Danny, Ellen, and Oakleigh go on after this? John's death has broken Howe Firehouse in a way that nothing else ever could break it.

This could be the end of Howe Firehouse as we know it.

This isn't the end of me and Carter. We're together. We'll always be together. Nothing can change that—not even a catastrophe at the end of the world.

Chapter 34:
Sophie

.

I walk down the stairs to the firehouse garage and find the crew waiting there for me. No one says a word. No one smiles. No one even makes eye contact with each other.

Billy gets behind the wheel of the rescue truck with Caleb in the seat next to him. Carter, Josh, and Vince sit in the middle seat. Jessie and I get into the back.

We're all wearing our uniforms and so are all our other crewmates manning the ladder truck and the two ambulances.

No one has seen or heard from Keith, Danny, Emily, Leila, or Ellen since John's death.

The firehouse has been running on fumes with the rest of us barely holding on and running calls the way we're supposed to. Someone has to protect this town. No one else is going to do it.

We drive downtown and Billy parks the truck in front of the First Presbyterian Church.

Hundreds of squad cars line the street. Uniformed Police officers direct the two trucks and the two ambulances to park right in front of the church.

A long line of black limousines sits parked there, too, along with the hearse.

Our crew unloads in numb silence. It's been like this ever since that disastrous barbecue.

Carter moves over next to me and takes my hand as we head inside. We make it halfway there before Ellis breaks away from the group.

"I can't do this!" he moans. "I can't go in there!"

We all turn around. Jessie goes over to him. "You have to come, Ellis. You can't miss John's funeral."

He breaks down wailing and wringing his hands. His face wrenches all over the place, but he's too anguished even to shed tears over this.

"He's dead because of me!" he chokes. "I'm the one who got him killed! He would be alive now if not for me."

"You can't tell yourself that." Jessie takes his hands and tries to straighten him out. "You didn't do this, Ellis. You didn't kill John. Andy did."

He barely hears her. "I can't go in there! I can't face Keith and Danny! Keith is gonna kill me!"

"No, he won't," Josh tells him. "No one blames you for this. I'm certain the Brewers don't."

"I can't do this!" Ellis whimpers and tries to tear himself out of Jessie's grip. "I can't face it!"

Jessie starts telling him again that he has to go. He's just starting to get hysterical and struggle against her grip when Carter steps in.

He pushes her out of the way, takes Ellis's hands, and moves in front of Ellis's face. Carter positions his eyes directly in line with Ellis's eyes so Ellis has no choice but to look at him.

I know that expression so well. No one can ignore Carter when he looks like that.

"Look at me, Ellis. Look at me!" Ellis's eyes snap to Carter's haunted face. Ellis doesn't look away this time.

"Listen to me, Ellis," Carter murmurs in an undertone. "I'm alive right now because of you. You saved my life and I admire you for that. Andy would have killed me and maybe even more of our crewmates if you hadn't acted when you did. You had no way of knowing John was standing behind me when the gun went off—but I do know one thing. John Brewer would have wanted you to save me even if he had known what was going to happen. He would have told you to save me. That's the kind of man he was. You saved my life by tackling me the way you did. I owe you forever for that. You're a hero in my book—and I know Keith and Danny feel the same way. Even Ellen feels that way. You know they do if you just think about it."

Ellis stares at him in shock and another dangerous silence falls over our group. I hear Naomi, Chris, and Brooke sobbing in the background.

Ellis's features spasm in agony. Poor guy.

Carter doesn't give him a second chance to back out of it. Carter lets go of Ellis's hands, puts his arm around Ellis's shoulders, and steers him toward the church.

Carter keeps his hold on Ellis, gives all of us a stern look, and we head up the driveway to the entrance.

Hundreds of people pack the church to bursting. People have to stand in the aisles to fit because there isn't enough room in the pews.

The mayor, the City Council members, and a bunch of other city big shots occupy the front pews.

The shiny black coffin sits on a pedestal in the center of the aisle. Mountains of flowers cover it and spill over onto the floor.

Uniformed Police officers line the walls and both sides of the aisle going all the way up to the altar.

The whole fire crew files past the coffin in two lines on either side of it. We climb up to the altar and stand at attention on both sides of the altar platform.

We flank the Brewer family. They sit in chairs on one side of the altar.

The whole family wears fancy black clothes. The men wear beautiful tailored black suits and all the women and girls wear nice dresses and hats.

The priest comes to the pulpit and starts talking about Heaven and reward and duty a whole lot of other crap.

The service goes on and on with most of the town dignitaries getting up and praising John Brewer for his service, professionalism, and selfless dedication.

I barely listen to anything they say. None of those fancy words can touch the sorrow and loss the fire crew is going through right now.

Keith sits in stone-faced silence staring straight in front of him. He sets his face in a granite wall of cold fury, clamps his mouth shut, and doesn't look sideways at anyone, not even his wife sitting right next to him.

Leila holds baby Leon in her arms. She has to keep moving him around, patting him on the back, and tending to all his needs while she dabs her eyes with a tissue every now and then.

Danny is an absolute wreck. His face and eyes have swollen up and turned bright red. He fights his features under control while silent tears streak down his cheeks through the whole service.

Ellen holds Oakleigh on her lap and hugs the girl. Oakleigh wails loudly through the whole service. She doesn't stop even once.

Ellen sobs quietly, too. Neither of them even tries to hold it together.

An elderly couple sits at the end of the line. I can only assume those are the Brewer brothers' parents. Both of them cry through the service. None of the family seems to be listening to anything anyone says.

The service eventually ends. Oakleigh breaks down screaming in anguish when Keith, Danny, Billy, Caleb, Josh, and George take hold of the coffin and carry it in procession out of the church.

The rest of the family follows all sobbing their eyes out. The fire crew follows next. I'm too numb from grief even to feel what's happening.

That box up there—that isn't John Brewer.

I don't know where John is. Maybe I'll go back to work and find him waiting for me at the firehouse. He has to be there. He's always there. Where else would he be?

The fire crew stands at attention while the pallbearers put the coffin in the hearse. Some people hug each other and then the family gets into the limos.

We climb back into the truck. The hearse starts slowly winding its way through the streets followed by the limos.

The two fire trucks and the two ambulances take the next position with a massive convoy of cop cars, other limos, and civilian cars trailing through town all the way to the graveyard.

People come out of their houses along the way and watch in silence as John Brewer takes his last ride to his final resting place.

When we get there, we go through another long process of people saying nice things about John before they lower the coffin into the hole.

Almost everyone on the crew breaks down crying when the family starts throwing dirt into the hole. The clods thud on top of the coffin.

Oakleigh's constant howling is really starting to get to me. It gets to everyone and Leon starts crying, too. Zeke slams his hands over his ears and his mother hugs him against her side. Danny doesn't even notice.

I wish I could cry for John Brewer—and for everything else this crew has lost over the years.

I don't know when the reality will hit, but it isn't hitting now. It might take a while.

Everyone on the fire crew comes forward to add dirt to the hole. Carter and I do the same thing, but not even that brings it home to me.

The service ends and still dozens upon dozens of people come forward to put dirt into the hole.

Those who have finished start to drift away. The crew stands around shuffling their feet until Billy mumbles, "We better get back. Come on."

We head back to the truck. The crowd around John's grave is just as thick as before.

I can't see the family anymore, but duty calls. Someone has to run Howe Firehouse. We could get another call any second now.

When that happens, we'll have to step up no matter how rotten we feel about John's death.

He would want us to keep going. He would want us to keep doing our jobs no matter what. The whole town is counting on us.

<u>End of Book 6.</u>

Keep Reading

Firehouse Blues Series: Book 7: Fire Chief

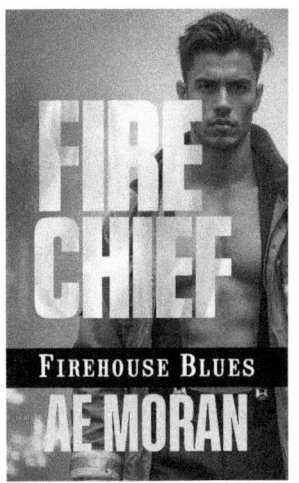

The brave firefighters and paramedics of Howe Fire Department are still reeling and barely able to cope after the tragic death of Fire Chief John Brewer. His brothers, Keith and Danny, are too grief-stricken to return to work. No one has seen or heard from them since the fatal shooting. Could this be the end of Howe Fire Department and the close bonds John worked so hard to build?

No one knows what to think when Duke Broebeck bursts onto the scene to fill John's shoes and pull the firehouse family back from the brink. Duke doesn't make any friends by flexing his authority and taking charge, but that might just be exactly what the firehouse needs right now.

Duke quickly earns the crew's respect. He might be as big a hero as John ever was, but things fall apart when circumstances threaten to derail Naomi McFee's career forever. A chain reaction of disasters and coincidences throw her and Duke together until neither of them can pretend they are only working together as boss and subordinate. These two lost souls will have to dig deep to find out what their lives and careers are really worth before Duke and Naomi lose everything.

You can find it at your favorite book retailer.

Get All of AE Moran's Free Books

S ign Up Once—Get all A.E. Moran's free books including brand new releases

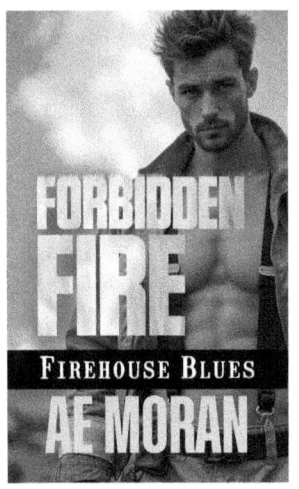

When what you want most is the one thing you can never have......

Austin McAuliffe is every woman's dream firefighter—young, strong, drop-dead hot, and selflessly dedicated to his career—and to the woman of his heart, Emma Brady. Only one other person holds a place in Austin's life—his best friend and fellow firefighter, Theo Gough. Austin insists on Theo spending time with Austin and Emma as a couple, especially when these two firefighters have a hard day at the office.

No one can believe when Austin completely flips out and randomly accuses Theo and Emma of flirting with each other in front of the whole fire crew. Could there be some deeper, more sinister reason for Austin to suddenly lose his mind and lash out at those closest to him?

Emma is devastated when Austin coldly dumps her with no warning and disappears out of her life, but Austin casts a long shadow. The nightmare of his sudden betrayal will come back to haunt Emma and Theo long after Austin is gone. Will the ghosts of the past ruin any chance for them to regain their happiness.....or will Austin's madness take down everyone he cares about along with him?

Sign up at www.authoraemoran.com to read it for free.

About AE Moran

A.E Moran is the contemporary romance pen name for Theo Mann.

I write 70 books per year—and yes, before you ask, all these books are my original creative work. Nothing written under my name is AI-generated or ghostwritten because I write better than AI and any ghostwriter out there.

People don't read fiction for entertainment or to escape from reality. People read fiction to see their humanity reflected in another person's character and story.

This is my promise to you. When you read my books, you'll see your own humanity reflected in the characters and stories. I take this commitment to my readers very seriously. My books are an intimate form of communication between us. I would never disrespect my readers by turning that over to a machine or another writer. This is my bond between me and you as my reader.

I write 20,000 words per day as my daily work output. If anyone with a public platform would like to challenge me to prove this in a controlled environment, feel free to contact me on this website's contact page.

I worked as a professional ghostwriter for fifteen years. Now I'm going for the Guinness World Record by writing 700 books over the next ten years and 1400 books over the next twenty years, all originally written by me. See my website for the full book list.

I'm also the author of *Proof for the Existence of God* and the *Crimes Against Fiction* blog. You can find all my nonfiction work at www.crimes-against-fiction.com.

If you have a story idea, or if you would like me to explore a series in more depth, or if you'd like me to explore a character by writing a spinoff series about that character or world, leave me a message on my website's contact page. I answer all reader emails, so ask me anything, tell me what you liked and didn't like, and let me know where you'd like your favorite series to go. I would love to hear your ideas and find out what you'd like to read next.

You can find out more at www.theomann.com or at www.authoraemoran.com.

Also by AE Moran (so far)

<u>Standalone Novels</u>

Heart on a Knife Edge

Dream Dimension

Just Friends

Back From the Dead

Damaged

Small Town Reunion

<u>Series</u>

Firehouse Blues (Books 1-10)

Turning Point Ranch (Books 1-10)

The Billionaires' Club (Books 1-10)

Paradise Cruises (Book 1-8)

Royal House (1-10)

Summerton Estates (1-10)